The Ostrich and Other Lost Things

Also by Beth Hautala

Waiting for Unicorns

The Ostrich and Other Lost Things

Beth Hautala

Philomel Books

PHILOMEL BOOKS
an imprint of Penguin Random House LLC
375 Hudson Street, New York, NY 10014

Library of Congress Cataloging-in-Publication Data
Names: Hautala, Beth, author.
Title: The ostrich and other lost things / Beth Hautala.
Description: New York, NY : Philomel Books, [2018] | Summary: Olivia,
eleven, has a knack for finding lost things, but when she promises her brother,
Jacob, that she will find his ostrich, she hopes its return will cure his autism. |
Identifiers: LCCN 2017023461 | ISBN 9780399546068 (hardback) |
ISBN 9780399546082 (e-book) | Subjects: | CYAC: Brothers and sisters—Fiction. |
Autism—Fiction. | Lost and found possessions—Fiction. | Zoo animals—
Fiction. | Family life—Oklahoma—Fiction. | Oklahoma—Fiction. |
BISAC: JUVENILE FICTION / Family / Siblings. | JUVENILE FICTION / Social
Issues / Special Needs. | JUVENILE FICTION / Animals / Zoos. |
Classification: LCC PZ7.H2886 Ost 2018 | DDC [Fic]—dc23
LC record available at https://lccn.loc.gov/2017023461

Printed in the United States of America.
ISBN 9780399546068
1 3 5 7 9 10 8 6 4 2

Edited by Liza Kaplan.
Design by Jennifer Chung.
Text set in 10-point FreightText Pro.

For my sisters, Amber and Erin,
champions of the Love Anyway—my first best friends.
Thank you for being the kind of women
who are all of their colors.

Prologue

I COULDN'T FIND my brother's ostrich.

I'd been trying for a long time. And I was extraordinarily good at finding things.

"You are extraordinarily good at finding things, Olivia," said Mom.

"It's your superpower," said Dad.

"Your superpower," said my brother. And then he said "superpower" for the rest of the day—repeating it over and over until the word no longer had any meaning and was just a bunch of sounds.

But superpower or not, Jacob's ostrich stayed missing. Despite how hard and long I searched.

"I'll find it, Jacob," I promised him. I wasn't done looking. It was our secret.

"That's okay, Olivia," he said.

But it wasn't.

He wasn't.

And as long as his ostrich stayed missing, I knew he would never be okay again.

1
....

Knowing and Finding

THE FIRST LOST thing I ever found was a ring Mom had gotten from Grandma. It was beautiful, all silver and swirls. And there were diamonds, too.

"I set it on this shelf, right here," Mom said to me, pointing at the narrow shelf that hung on the wall by the hall mirror. "And now it's gone!" She rubbed the empty place on her finger where the ring should have been, but wasn't. "I can't think what I did with it. I've looked everywhere."

Mom's face told me something about lost things that day: Lost things matter. Sometimes even more because they're lost.

When you're searching for lost things, you have to change the way you're thinking. You can't just look for the item you've lost. You have to look for what things are not where they belong. Mom's ring had fallen off the shelf and rolled before coming to a stop just out of sight under the hall-closet door. I found it down on my hands and knees with my cheek pressed to the floor, scanning for anything that might be out of place.

So many things go missing. And I've always been good at

finding them. I guess it's because I'm pretty observant. Sometimes I even find things before their owners realize they're missing. Especially things in weird places. Like car keys in the fruit bowl on the kitchen counter instead of in their usual spot in the bowl by the door. Dad's wallet on the bookshelf in the hall instead of on his nightstand. Mom's purse hanging on the back of the kitchen chair instead of on the hook by the door. Library books in the bathroom. Earrings in the junk drawer. Jacob's favorite pencil mixed in with the silverware. But whatever the item, it's much easier for a thing to get lost than it is to be found. That's why finding things feels so good.

I saw the piece of paper in the window before I even looked at the clock.

"I'm going across the street!" I called down the hall, and went in search of my shoes.

"Good morning to you, too," Mom laughed. "You want toast or cereal for breakfast?"

"Toast," I said. "I'll be back in a minute." I closed the front door behind me and then opened it again and poked my head back inside. "And good morning."

Mom shook her head and waved me off.

I glanced up at Mrs. Mackenelli's front window as I skipped up her steps. The paper was my signal. She'd lost her glasses again. It happened so often, we'd decided a signal would be a good idea so she didn't have to call every time she needed me. If the paper was in the window, I'd pull on my shoes and head across the street. Sometimes even before I'd changed out of my pajamas or eaten breakfast.

"Hello, dear!"

Mrs. Mackenelli usually called me dear. Or Olivia Dear. She closed the door behind me. Orion was purring in his green wing-back chair on the other side of the living room. "Thank you for coming."

"Sure!" I smiled and looked around the room, searching for clues.

"Have you had breakfast?"

I shook my head. "I'll eat when I get home."

"Coffee then?"

I grinned.

"I'll go put the pot on." And she winked.

Mrs. Mackenelli let me drink coffee whenever I came over to help her find her glasses. I don't think Mom knew. She probably would have said I shouldn't because eleven isn't old enough. But Mrs. Mackenelli didn't seem to think that mattered, so we both drank coffee whenever I came over.

"Okay, so what were you doing last night?" I asked. I had a couple of guesses—TV, for one. There was a pillow standing upright against the couch cushion where she'd been sitting. But even though I was good at collecting clues, it couldn't hurt to ask if there was anything else I should know.

"Well, Orion and I watched the nine o'clock news together, as we usually do. But the weather report bothered him, so I turned it off early. I still had my glasses then."

I nodded.

"After that we went to the kitchen for our nightcap." Mrs. Mackenelli called milk her "nightcap," I think because it helped her fall asleep. There were two drinking glasses in the sink. One for Mrs. Mackenelli and one for Orion. I looked around the kitchen, but there was no sign of the missing glasses.

"Then what did you do?"

"I washed my face and went to bed," she said. "I was going to read for a little while first, but I couldn't find my glasses."

"So, somewhere between your nightcap and washing your face, your glasses disappeared."

Mrs. Mackenelli nodded, and I closed my eyes, gathering all the clues in my mind. Where would I have taken off my glasses, if I were her? I backtracked through the kitchen and stared at the empty cups in the sink. Then over to the living room, where the couch and TV sat. And then, just like that, I knew where they were. The glasses were pulling at me, like an itch on the inside of my brain. I walked back into the kitchen, opened the refrigerator, and sure enough, there they were. Right next to the carton of milk.

I pulled them out and handed them to Mrs. Mackenelli. She took them, shook her head, and smiled.

"You are a wonder, Olivia," she said.

I shrugged and stuffed my hands into my pockets. I was hardly a wonder. Mostly it just felt good to be helpful. And I was happy to do something completely normal that had nothing to do with my brother, Jacob.

"You probably would have found your glasses as soon as you went to the fridge for cream," I said, glancing at the coffeepot. "I was just one step ahead of you."

"Well, you usually are, my dear." She set down a cup of coffee in front of me, and I filled it up with cream and sugar until it was the color of Orion's front paws.

I ran back across the street to our house, which stretched out across the lawn like a cat in the morning sunshine. All one level, white with green shutters.

"How'd it go?" Mom called. I let the screen door slam behind me—once, twice, three times before coming to a close.

"Found 'em!" I kicked off my shoes and padded barefoot into the kitchen.

"Of course you did." Mom smiled and set my breakfast on the table. "You always do." Her voice was firm and convincing, like it usually was when she talked to me. But she was good at changing her voice—and her face—depending on whom she was talking to. She had a telephone voice, and a voice she used when talking to Dad. She had a friend voice, a work voice, a voice for Jacob, and a voice for me.

Jacob was already at the table with his breakfast—a measuring cup full of cereal, a measuring cup full of milk, two empty bowls, a glass of orange juice, and two spoons. Eating was kind of like a game for Jacob. It all happened in his head before it happened in his mouth, so everything had to be a certain way.

I sat down at the table with my peanut-butter-and-banana toast and watched my brother.

Into the first empty bowl went half a cup of dry cereal and then half a cup of milk. He ate with his right hand. Carefully. Slowly. And then he drank half his orange juice. When he finished, he pushed the bowl and spoon aside, wiped his mouth on his napkin, and then took the second bowl and repeated the process. Only this time he used his left hand. I didn't interrupt because that just made him upset. Instead I watched. Just like I do every morning. And when he was finished eating, he picked up his dirty dishes and brought them to the sink. Just like usual.

"Good morning, Olivia," he said finally. And the way he said it made you believe it was. He said my name carefully. Like it was important. Like it mattered.

"Good morning, Jacob," I said. "Tell me something I've never heard before." This was our routine.

My brother grinned. "Did you know the teeth of the American beaver never stop growing? They must chew wood constantly to keep their teeth from growing out of their mouths and into their lips."

I ran my tongue across my teeth. "I didn't know that, Jacob. Thank you," I said.

"You're welcome." He nodded and left the table.

Jacob loved telling us new facts, and he did so a lot because he was very good at remembering things. But you could never really be sure what Jacob might tell you. Sometimes it was a pretty normal fact about the weather. Like that it rained thirty-seven inches in Prue last year. Other times he'd say something like, "Did you know elephants poop about three hundred pounds every day?" Or "Did you know that if the earth suddenly stopped spinning, everything on the surface of the earth would suddenly be moving at sixteen hundred kilometers per hour? Even the oceans would slosh sideways that fast." Jacob knew a lot of things, and I liked learning from him. If I ever needed to know some random fact or bit of interesting information, I could count on Jacob. He was especially good at science, and he even used to help me with homework sometimes. But you never knew what he'd share with people. Which is why we played this game at breakfast and not at dinner. Sometimes we had people over for dinner, and it was hard for some people to appreciate random facts like the growth rate of beaver teeth or the daily weight of elephant poop or the speed of a sideways-sloshing ocean if they weren't used to hearing about those kinds of things. But we were used to it. We were used to Jacob.

We had to be.

Remembering random facts was Jacob's superpower. He had been knowing things for as long as I had been finding lost objects. And most of the time we made a pretty good team.

Most of the time.

2

No Lions

A WEEK LATER, I sat down to breakfast, and before I could even pour my cereal, Jacob said, "Did you know today will be the hottest Tuesday of the year so far?"

"No, I didn't know that, Jacob," I said. "Thank you."

"You're welcome," he said. Like always. And then he went to get ready for school, even though summer vacation had started last week.

Change was hard for him.

Mom said it was okay to let Jacob stick to his old routines because it helped to keep him in the swing of things. So, Jacob got ready for school, even though there was no school to go to, and then we walked to the zoo. It wasn't the zoo we'd grown up going to in the city, though—just a tiny part of a zoo that Prue got for the summer. Practically in our backyard.

Zoos don't usually move around, but the state of Oklahoma didn't want to close the zoo completely during the renovations they were doing. So, the exhibits were broken into sections, assigned to different towns, and moved across the state in giant semi trucks and trailers. Like a deck of cards passed around Oklahoma. I felt bad for the animals being torn away from each other like that, but I was also curious to see which exhibits had come to Prue.

"The Tulsa Zoo Coming to You!" Their slogan was on billboards and posters, TV, and radio. It was a really catchy jingle, especially with the music. Like one of those tunes that got stuck in your head. What did Dad call it? An earworm. The tune was stuck in my head, and I hummed it while Jacob and I walked.

Prue's piece of the Tulsa Zoo was moving right to the edge of a corner of state land less than a mile walk from our backyard. It hadn't officially opened yet, so I wanted to go and watch the animals get unloaded.

"I don't think anyone will mind if you just stand and watch," Mom had said. "But I was planning to work out in the garden this morning, so you and Jacob will have to go on your own. Okay?"

Jacob and I didn't spend that much time out of the house just the two of us. Mom usually came, too, in case he needed help.

But I said okay, and off we went. I was glad that Mom trusted me to handle things, but a little nervous, too.

My brother was so excited, he hurried ahead of me all the way to the gate. And Jacob never hurried.

The dusty ground radiated heat through my sneakers, and the high-pitched, singsong rasping of the cicadas filled the morning air with the sounds of summer. It was the end of May, but it was hot.

Just like Jacob had said it would be. Even at nine o'clock in the morning.

"Lions and tigers and bears, oh MY! Lions and tigers and bears, oh MY!" Jacob chanted the phrase over and over as we walked. And then he shortened it to just "Lions and tigers! Lions and tigers! Lions and tigers!" until all the words blended together.

His excitement was contagious, and I chanted along with him. I couldn't wait to see the animals. I hoped there would be zebras and elephants.

But as we got closer, I saw there was a sign on the gate:

NOT OPEN TO THE PUBLIC

I didn't feel like "the public"—I didn't feel like the words on that sign were meant for me, or for my brother, but we stood behind the closed gate like we were supposed to. There were lots of trucks in the makeshift parking lot, and we watched the zoo staff unload equipment as they set up their temporary home. Once some large, tall fences were in place, the animals were unloaded one at a time from a variety of cages and vehicles.

First came the monkeys, which were especially loud. My brother covered his ears when they started screeching.

Then three donkeys. It took four people to get the last one out of its trailer because it refused to move.

"Ha!" Jacob laughed. "Olivia, look! Look at the donkey!"

Then there was a giant tortoise. It was so big I could have ridden on it.

After that came a Komodo dragon, which was pretty exciting. Everyone was treating that lizard with a lot of respect. Which made sense. It probably could have eaten me in just a couple bites.

After the Komodo dragon came out, though, I got a little nervous. There was only one trailer left to unload, and so far we'd struck out. This last truck wasn't big enough for elephants. Or tigers, bears, or zebras, really. Maybe it could hold lions? It was hard to think with the monkeys screaming and screeching in their cages, jumping up and down and adding to the expectation and anxiety.

I could tell Jacob was nervous, too; I knew the signs. He rubbed his arms and hugged himself tightly as we stood under the hot sun, repeating "lions, lions, lions" over and over. He shifted his weight back and forth from one foot to the other, looking everywhere except at me.

Another sign.

I really didn't want Jacob to have a meltdown, so I needed to be ready to do something if they didn't bring a lion out of that trailer.

"Hey Jacob," I said. "Don't you think Komodo dragons are awesome? I mean, they *are* dragons."

Jacob relaxed a tiny bit.

"There are no such things as dragons, Olivia."

"Are you sure?" I asked. It helped to play along.

"Yes. I'm sure." Jacob quit rocking. He couldn't believe I didn't know this. "The Komodo dragon is a lizard. The heaviest lizard on earth, but not the biggest. It can run up to eleven miles per hour in short bursts. Unlike mythological dragons, it doesn't fly or breathe fire. But it is a carnivore and will overpower its prey with sheer strength and serrated teeth."

When Jacob shared facts, it often sounded like he was reading from an encyclopedia. I just nodded, listening and watching him.

"Most people think the Komodo dragon poisons people with its saliva. But that is a myth. The Komodo dragon poisons its prey with venom. Toxins lower blood pressure, cause massive bleeding, prevent clotting, and induce shock."

"Oh." I stared at him for a minute. "That's kinda gross, Jacob."

"That's kinda gross, Jacob," he said, repeating my words. He did that sometimes when he was nervous or worried. Sometimes even when he was excited.

Finally, they opened the last trailer. One of the zoo staff walked inside cautiously.

Let it be a lion . . . let it be a lion . . . let it be a lion . . . But when the staff person came back out, what marched behind him down the ramp was definitely not a lion. It was a large-eyed, long-necked ostrich.

My brother froze.

I froze.

And then suddenly Jacob wasn't frozen anymore. He was looking everywhere except at the giant bird. He began swaying and rocking, twisting his shirtsleeves and humming anxiously. Then Jacob collapsed in the dust and started wailing.

"Waaaaaaaaaaaa!"

I crouched down beside him. "Okay, Jacob," I said. "Time to go home."

Nothing.

I rubbed his back, but he just shook me off. "I know you're upset," I soothed. "So am I. I wish there were lions, too. Ostriches make me upset, too." That last part was a lie. "But crying isn't going to fix anything." That part was true.

Jacob just screamed.

"This is the worst day ever!" my brother yelled through tears.

I rolled my eyes. "Really? Worst day ever?" I was getting frustrated. "Seriously, Jacob. I can think of a whole lot worse days than this—"

"NO!" His voice rose an octave and cut me off. I glanced around. One of the zoo staff stopped what she was doing and stood watching us from the other side of the gate.

"Hey, Jacob, how about we pretend we're in a jungle and we need to run home before the jungle animals catch us?" We used to play this game a lot when we were little. Jacob was always a panther, and I was usually a bird of some kind. It was fun.

But Jacob didn't want to play. He only shrieked and yelled. So,

I tried again. I tried all the things I usually did, plus all the things I'd seen Mom and Dad try.

I lowered my voice and did my best to stay calm. "Come on, Jacob. Let's go home, okay?"

"No! No! No! GO!" Jacob screamed at me.

I stood up and took a deep breath. This was only getting worse. I couldn't do this. Not here. Not by myself.

"Everything all right?" The woman behind the gate approached, her face a mix of concern and suspicion.

"Yeah! It's fine!" I smiled a big happy smile and gritted my teeth. "My brother's just a little upset. Sorry—"

"WHY DO YOU HAVE MY OSTRICH?" Jacob screamed.

"Uh—" The woman's look of concern shifted to confusion, and her face turned red.

"WHY DO YOU HAVE MY OSTRICH?" Jacob screamed even louder, his despair shifting to anger.

"Easy, kid." She was frowning now.

But Jacob wouldn't calm down. He stood up and balled his fists. He was taller than I was. And strong. His face was as red as the woman's behind the gate. I was glad there was something separating us from one another.

I ignored the woman and cautiously slipped my hand into Jacob's, giving it a little squeeze. Normally Jacob didn't like when people touched him. Even Mom and Dad. But it was different with me. It had always been different.

"Come on, Jacob. Please? I need you to take me home now."

He took a shuddering breath and glanced in my direction. The woman at the gate watched.

"Take me home, Jacob? I can't remember the way." I tugged on my brother's hand like a little kid might do. Jacob rocked back and forth, trying to catch his breath from crying. After a few moments, he finally nodded and turned away from the gate.

"It's all right, Olivia," he said. He took another deep, shuddering breath. "I remember the way."

So, I let him lead me, my hand still in his, like I was the one who needed help.

As we walked away, I turned back for one last look at the animals. The woman in the uniform was still standing behind the gate. And she stayed there, watching us, like we were the ones in a cage.

3
....

One Hundred Percent Done

AS FAR BACK as I could remember, Jacob had always had meltdowns. Whenever he was tired or scared or nervous. When he didn't like what Mom was making for dinner. When his favorite TV show wasn't on that night. But after his toy ostrich disappeared six months ago, everything got worse.

My brother's ostrich was small. Only about three or four inches tall and made of hard plastic. A perfect copy of the real thing. And Jacob loved it. It used to go everywhere with him. He'd hold it up to the car window whenever we drove anywhere so it could look out. It sat at the breakfast table with us in the morning so that Jacob could feed it bits of cereal. He even used to keep it perched on his nightstand as he slept.

That little toy bird was Jacob's most important thing. And when he lost it, all the little things that made Jacob seem different suddenly turned into big things. He got upset more often, and his meltdowns got worse. It became harder to calm him down, too. It was like that little toy ostrich had steadied Jacob—had helped keep all the pieces of him together somehow. And lately it seemed like

Dad and Mom and me were spending more and more time trying to keep Jacob from falling apart.

I needed to find that ostrich.

Sweat dripped down my back, making my T-shirt stick to me the whole walk home. There was dust in my teeth, and I wanted a glass of water more than anything.

I squinted and watched the heat rise up in shimmering waves over the dirt road ahead of us. Horseflies buzzed around, landing every now and then, and biting. Jacob was still holding my hand. I shook him off twice, because I wanted to hurry up and get home— out of the sun, away from the flies, and away from this morning that had not gone as planned.

But both times Jacob reached down and grabbed my hand right back. And because I didn't want him to get upset again, I held hands with my brother. All the way home. Only this time he didn't hurry.

It took forever, but we finally made it.

"I am one hundred percent done," I said as I walked into the kitchen. The screen door slammed shut behind me. It bounced in its frame a couple of times before coming to a close. Jacob remained outside on the porch where I'd left him. He would never come through a door unless someone told him he could.

Mom glanced at Jacob out on the porch, and then at me, and matched my folded arms.

"Well. Okay." She looked at me from over the rim of her glasses.

"Mom! He has a meltdown every time one little thing doesn't go the way he expects!" Jacob was still standing out on the porch and I knew he could hear me, but I didn't care.

"It was that bad?" Mom's forehead wrinkled.

"Yes. And worse."

She cleared her throat and nodded toward Jacob like she wanted to remind me he was listening. Mom had a pretty big no-sass-be-kind policy, and I knew I was pushing it. I took a deep breath and tried to calm down.

"So," she said, "would you say your own expectations weren't met?"

I rolled my eyes. My deep breaths weren't working. "Just for once I'd like to do something and not have to worry about Jacob! Just once I'd like to not have him fall apart over the stupidest things! I just wish—I just—"

"You just wish what?"

I let out a big sigh. "Nothing. Never mind."

"You just wish what, Olivia?"

"NOTHING! I SAID NEVER MIND. It doesn't matter!"

"Attitude. Room, please. Now." Mom pointed and I went. I even stomped a little. Inside it felt like someone had squeezed me too tight. She hadn't heard me. She hadn't heard what I'd been trying to say. What I couldn't say. She never heard me. Jacob was the one Mom listened to—to everything he said, and everything he didn't say.

I flopped across my bed. I kicked off my shoes and stared at my ceiling fan, trying to focus on just one blade until it seemed like I could slow the whole thing down or speed it up with my mind.

I just wish Jacob was different, more normal—like before. I wish we all were. But I couldn't tell Mom that.

Slowly, as I stared up at the ceiling fan, all the mad fell out of me, like sand pouring out of shoes.

We all knew Jacob was not like other kids his age, even before he was diagnosed with autism. He was thirteen years old, but parts of his brain sometimes made him seem like only five or six. He got upset over things that didn't matter to most people. He did weird stuff like not going through doors without being told he could, or only eating certain foods a certain way. Sometimes he copied what people around him were saying, and he had trouble making eye contact. Loud noises bothered him, and bright lights, and too many people talking at once, and he really didn't like when we drove fast. He couldn't stand the feel of grass against his bare feet or tags on his clothes, either. He never sang anymore, but he did hum, and he loved music. We used to play ring-around-the-rosy over and over, spinning in circles in the backyard until we were so dizzy we couldn't stand.

Jacob had always liked knowing things and telling people about them in his steady breathless way of talking—like he had to get all his words out in one long stream in case any of them got lost on the way. And he'd always rocked and twisted his shirtsleeves whenever he got upset or scared. But lately, it had become harder to help Jacob, so he was going to therapy on a more regular basis. His differences were becoming more and more noticeable.

I was starting to feel a little dizzy from staring at the ceiling fan for so long when Mom knocked on my door and opened it a crack.

"Hey," she said.

"Hey." I made room for her on the bed. She flopped down beside me, and we both stared up at the spinning blades for a few minutes, not saying anything.

"I'm sorry I wasn't there, Olivia."

I sighed. "It probably wouldn't have mattered if you had been. There was an ostrich."

"An ostrich!"

I nodded.

"Oh." She said it slowly, like things made more sense now.

"Yeah."

"Well, I'm still sorry I wasn't there to handle your brother."

"It's okay," I said. "Maybe it's better you weren't. Sometimes he gets worse for you."

Mom didn't say anything, and I instantly regretted what I had said. It was true, but I could tell right away it hurt her feelings.

"Look, I know things aren't always so easy, and I know you've had a lot more to deal with, with your brother, than a lot of kids. But I do know that as hard as it is, Jacob needs you." Mom smiled at me. "You're a great sister to him. And I know he loves you very much. Even if he can't tell you or show you like your dad and I can."

Sure, Jacob needed me. But I wasn't sure if Mom was entirely right. Did Jacob even know how to love? Was love still love if a person didn't tell you—or *couldn't* tell you? Were there other ways to show people you loved them?

It was tiring to think about, and I wanted to be done talking about this. "I'm sorry, too. I shouldn't have yelled," I said. I stared at the side of my mom's face. She rolled over and kissed me on the nose.

"I love you," she said. "Even when you yell."

"I love you, too," I said.

Mom was the kind of person who was pretty up close and far away. Her eyes were brown with little bits of green mixed in, and her lashes were so thick and dark that if she didn't put makeup on, you'd never know. I'd always wished I looked like her. But I didn't. Jacob did. I looked like my dad, with his curly red hair and grey eyes.

"I have to get groceries," she said. "Want to come?"

"Is Jacob coming?" It was a stupid question because Jacob always came everywhere. We couldn't just leave him alone.

Mom gave me a look.

I sighed again. "I guess I'll come."

She sat up and gave my knee a squeeze. "Good. I like your company. And your face."

I laughed. "I like your face, too."

. . . . .

County Market was about a ten-mile drive from our house, but if you took the back roads, it could stretch to almost twenty. And that was what we did, because Jacob didn't like driving fast.

He was in the backseat, right in the middle, with all the seat belts buckled around him—the lap belt and both shoulder belts. Mom just smiled at him in the rearview mirror.

"You look very safe, Jacob."

"Did you know that lap and shoulder seat belts reduce the risk of fatal injury by forty-five percent and reduce the risk of moderate-to-critical injury by fifty percent?"

"No, I didn't know that. Thank you, Jacob," Mom said.

"You're welcome," said my brother.

I tightened my seat belt up front.

Mom's grocery list wasn't long—milk, bread, eggs, some fruit and vegetables, and deli meat for the sandwiches Dad took to work every day. She stopped at a bin of green peppers and I picked up a few, examining several before choosing one and dropping it into the bag she held open for me.

We filled the basket in record time, and while Mom checked out, I went to see what sorts of lost things I could locate by the soda machines. I usually found loose change that had rolled just out of sight. Sometimes it seemed like I could feel the lostness of those coins, small and cold against my mind. But today there was nothing. Someone must have swept under the machines recently, because when I got down on my hands and knees—real quick so no one would notice—I didn't even see dust bunnies.

I walked over to the store's community bulletin board that hung against the wall. Business cards and want ads, pictures of missing pets and upcoming community events were pinned everywhere. I studied the missing pet pictures extra carefully, because chances were, I'd hear from some of their owners sooner or later. That's what happens when you live in a small town and you're extraordinarily good at finding lost things. But today there was more than just want ads and pictures of missing pets. Today there was also a small poster pinned to the upper right-hand corner of the board.

Tulsa Performing Arts Center

&

The Ramshackle Traveling Children's Theater Company

Present:

PETER PAN

Performances July 15—July 20

Auditions June 8 at 3 p.m. at the Tulsa Performing Arts Center

Children of all ages welcome

I sucked my breath between my teeth and let it out real slow. My stomach started jumping around so hard I actually folded my arms across my body, trying to settle it down.

"*Peter Pan*. Auditions June eighth. Children of all ages welcome." I whispered the words out loud to myself until I had everything memorized. Then I pulled off one of the little perforated tabs at the bottom of the poster that had a phone number and the name of the theater company on it. I slipped it into my pocket—more precious than any coin I might have found.

This was my chance.

Before Jacob lost his ostrich, we used to put on shows for Mom and Dad all the time. Things didn't always go as planned because Jacob liked to do his own thing, but it was still fun to pretend. And sometimes Jacob's version made our performances even better. One summer I even convinced my best friend, Becka, to do a talent show with us. We hung sheets over the garage doorway so we could open and close the curtain between performances. It wasn't professional, but it was exciting, and I loved performing.

The only real play I'd ever been in was a second-grade end-of-year school performance of *The Wizard of Oz*. All the elementary classes had to participate. I got to play the part of a poppy in the scene where Dorothy and her friends are lulled to sleep in the field before they reach Oz. Mostly I just stood there and swayed a little, but I'd loved every minute. The feel of the stage under my feet and the buzz of the audience before the curtain lifted. The heat of the lights, the rush of excitement, the thunder of applause at the end. There was just something about performing, about being on a stage. Something magical. It was a kind of pretending everyone agreed to believe. You got to be someone else, and everyone let you become that person.

After Jacob was diagnosed, it was hard to be anything other than his sister. Even a couple years ago, when Mom and Dad had agreed to an extracurricular, Jacob and I joined 4H together, and working on projects with him was fun. But lately, any extra activity at all, even if Jacob wasn't involved in it, was just too much. Like soccer this past spring. I wasn't very good, but it was fun to play, and I got to hang out with friends at practice after school. But there were a lot of practices, and games almost every Saturday; Jacob got nervous watching the ball fly around, and being around so many people all the time, and riding in the car more than usual. So, after the season ended, Mom and Dad said the family needed a break. No more "extra" things for a while.

But a play was different. It didn't last nearly as long as a soccer season, and Jacob wouldn't have to come to rehearsals because Mom could just drop me off. Plus, performances were just for one week at the beginning of August, and Jacob would only have to sit in the audience once—maybe twice.

This was different from soccer for another reason, too. I absolutely loved *Peter Pan*. I'd read the book over and over. I'd watched every version of every movie ever made. And I already knew exactly what part I wanted. Not that I'd definitely be cast as Wendy. But even if I wasn't, a Lost Boy or a pirate would be better than nothing. Finally, there was something I could do just for me. I could be in a play on my own, and I wouldn't have to worry about my brother.

The Wizard of Oz had been great, but Peter Pan would be even better—if I could convince Mom and Dad to let me try out.

I rubbed my fingers over the slip of paper in my pocket and thought about the play the whole ride home. What my costume would be like if I got the part of Wendy. A nightgown-dress kind of thing because Wendy and her brothers leave for Neverland at night when they are supposed to be sleeping. My hair was wrong—I didn't usually think of Wendy as having red hair—but hopefully that wouldn't matter. And maybe there would be actual flying! I wondered if Tinkerbell would be more of an imagined character instead of a person. A person-sized fairy didn't seem right somehow.

It was all so exciting.

I took a deep breath before I spoke. Jacob hummed to himself in the backseat.

"Mom? There's a community theater company doing a production of Peter Pan in Tulsa."

"Oh, yeah?" Her voice sounded kind of stiff.

"Yes," I said. "Auditions are next Wednesday at three p.m. And performances are in August—just for one week. And I really, really, *really* want to audition."

Mom didn't say anything. I could tell by the look on her face that she was thinking about things that were extra.

"I know after soccer you said no extra things for a little while because it's hard with Jacob and everything, but maybe you could just think about it? Please? Especially because it's summer? We don't have as much going on right now."

Mom stayed quiet. She didn't even look at me. She just gripped the steering wheel a little tighter and sighed.

"Just think about it?" I said softly. "It's important."

"I don't know, Olivia."

"Please? Just thi—"

"All right. I'll think about it," she said. Her words said maybe, but the tone of her voice said no.

I took another breath and stared out the window. On the inside, my heart felt hot. I tried not to do or say or even think anything more. It wouldn't help, and I didn't want to cry, because making a big deal about stuff just made everything worse. Jacob made a big deal about everything all the time, and it only made things harder for everyone.

So, I didn't bring up *Peter Pan* again for the rest of the ride, and when we got home, I pulled that little slip of paper from my pocket and looked at it, just for a second, before dropping it into the trash can.

4

....

Not Forgotten

I SAT IN my room and tried to forget about the play—about being Wendy, and the rush of being onstage. When I closed my eyes, all I could see was Jacob flailing on the ground in front of the zoo gate the way he had that morning. Or sitting buckled up with every seat belt strapped around him.

Jacob and I were so different.

But Mom was right—he needed me. And I needed that play. I had to help Jacob get better; I had to find his toy ostrich. I'd looked every day at first, but I hadn't been able to find it. Now it seemed crucial that I start looking again.

I grabbed my flashlight from the drawer in my nightstand and went outside.

There was a wooden board covering the opening of our porch's crawl space to keep skunks and rabbits and stray cats from getting in. I pulled away the board, crouched down, and turned on my flashlight. The beam of brightness cut through the darkness, traced only with dusty light that fell between the floorboards over my head. It was like another world under there. Damp and musty, cluttered with old leaves and dirt, mostly. Plus some pinecones and spiderwebs. Were there other animals hiding? Mice? Rats? Would I find old bones? Or maybe a toy ostrich.

I took a deep breath and wiggled through the crawl space on my stomach. It would be a strange place for Jacob to lose his ostrich, so I hadn't thought to check here until now. But didn't most lost things end up in strange places?

A cobweb stuck to the side of my face and I swiped it away, trying not to panic. I swept the beam from the flashlight toward the back wall under the porch, but I didn't see anything unusual.

"Olivia! Olivia?" Mom's voice carried through the floorboards overhead, muffled and far away inside the house. There was no point in answering. She wouldn't hear me. I shone my flashlight all around, into every corner. There *was* something stuck in the dirt, partially buried on the far right side. I couldn't make out what it was, so I crawled closer—elbows, knees, stomach to the ground.

"Olivia?" Mom yelled louder. The front screen door opened, and she stepped out onto the porch, almost directly overhead.

"Here! I'm, uh, I'm down here."

"Olivia?" She paused. "Are you under the porch?" Her voice sounded confused. And then amused. "What on earth are you doing under there?"

"I'm looking for something," I said.

"Like the opportunity to do some laundry?"

I rolled my eyes. She was right, though. My clothes were going to be filthy.

I stretched my arm as far as it could reach, and was just able to grab the thing I couldn't identify. A small plastic card. I rubbed the dirt off and held it up to my flashlight. A driver's license. Mom's driver's license. One she'd lost several months ago.

"I found your old driver's license," I called up to her.

"My old what?"

"Your driver's license." I swept my flashlight across the darkness of the crawl space one last time. There was nothing else under here. I crawled my way back toward the square patch of light. Mom's feet appeared in the opening, and then her face as she crouched down and stared into the darkness. I clicked off my flashlight and stuffed it into my pocket as I emerged back into the sunlight. Everything was suddenly very bright.

"Here." I handed her the driver's license and stood up, brushing dirt from my clothes and shaking dust out of my hair.

"Wow." Mom stared at the card in her hand and then at me.

"How do you think that got under there?" I asked.

She rubbed it between her fingers, thinking.

"I dropped my purse one day," she said. "A while ago. Everything fell out all over the porch. This must have fallen between the cracks in the floorboards. I replaced it and forgot all about the old one. I look so different!"

She laughed and held out the card so I could see. She did look different.

I smiled at her funny haircut and serious look in the picture. "It's still you, though," I said.

"Hmm." She smiled. "Lost or found—still the same." She reached out and brushed a smudge of dirt from my cheek. "Now. You, young lady, should head directly to the shower. Lunch is waiting when you're finished."

She pointed me in the direction of the bathroom, past Jacob, who was doing a puzzle at the kitchen table, but her eyes lingered on the lost ID in her hand. "Whatever possessed you to look under the porch?"

I wasn't sure how to respond. "Just good to look for missing things in unusual places every once in a while," I said. "You never know what you'll find."

She squinted at me. "Honey," her voice changed. "You are excellent at finding missing things. I love that you're always helping Mrs. Mackenelli find her glasses, and helping your dad and me, and Jacob, too."

"And Jacob, too," Jacob repeated.

I did my best to ignore him. Still, I couldn't ignore the "but" I heard in Mom's words. I didn't understand where she was going with this.

"I love finding lost things," I said.

"I know." Mom paused. "But maybe you don't have to try so hard? I just want to make sure you know that if you can't find something, that's okay, too."

"I know," I said. I'd become very good at *not* finding Jacob's ostrich.

Mom looked at me again for a minute before she spoke. "Okay, good." Another pause. "It's just that your dad and I have noticed that you've been spending a lot of time alone lately. Maybe too much time. I know Becka is gone for the summer, but—"

"Sometimes it's easier to do things alone. And to look for things by myself. It's not like there's a ton of stuff to do around here, especially because doing anything extra is so hard." I glanced up at her and thought about that slip of paper sitting in the trash. "But . . . if I could try out for that play, then I'd be doing stuff with lots of other kids."

Mom sighed. She looked tired. "Just promise me you won't put so much pressure on yourself. Especially with looking for lost items. I bet most people don't even realize half the things they've lost are even gone!"

I knew she was trying to make me feel better, but for some reason, what she said made me want to cry. If Mom was right, and people lost things all the time without ever even realizing they were missing, could some things just disappear and stay forgotten forever?

Even if that were true, I had to keep looking for Jacob's ostrich. I knew he wouldn't forget it, and I couldn't, either. It was too important.

I walked to the bathroom without another word to Mom, turned the shower to hot, and stepped right in.

5

....

Another Visit

LAST YEAR, MY teacher, Mr. Larson, assigned *Peter Pan* for one of our book reports. We also read *Romeo and Juliet*, *Tom Sawyer*, *The Jungle Book*, and a few others. The cool part was that we read the books aloud in class. We all thought it was a dumb idea at first. Our teachers had pretty much quit reading aloud to us after third grade. But because it was part of a literature section we were working through, Mr. Larson insisted we read it aloud. He wanted us to practice oral presentation. So, each kid got a turn to read a chapter to the class.

The book version of *Peter Pan* was way different from the movie, but I liked it better. I especially loved the idea of Neverland as a place for lost things and lost people. A place where you could belong and have fantastic adventures and forget you'd ever been lost before.

Peter was lost and couldn't get found. He had always been locked out when all he wanted was to belong. And nothing I'd read before had ever made me quite as sad as that. So, I left my window open from time to time. Just in case.

·····

Later that afternoon, Jacob started wailing in his bedroom. I heard Mom go in to ask him what was wrong, and I heard Jacob answer that he was frustrated. He couldn't get his shirts hung up in the closet just right. He was hysterical about it.

I couldn't tune it out, so I pulled my copy of *Peter Pan* from my bookshelf and flipped through it. The pages were dog-eared in the places I liked best. I'd underlined stuff and even made notes in the margins. It would be nice to reread some of my favorite passages. And maybe if Mom saw me carrying the book, she'd realize I was extra serious about wanting to audition for the play.

I held my copy of *Peter Pan* in one hand and a package of Starburst in the other. Starburst was my most favorite candy ever.

"I'm going outside!" I shouted.

"Where to?" Mom shouted back. She was cutting up vegetables for stir-fry. Not my favorite dinner.

I walked into the kitchen. "Just down the road. I want to go look at the zoo again."

"Really?" Mom turned around from her spot at the counter.

"Yeah," I said. "I just want another look. By myself."

Mom nodded, but she looked confused, and I couldn't really explain it. I didn't know why I wanted to go back. I just needed to be by myself, out of the house, for a little while. I needed to get away from things that felt like they were the way they were—the way they *had* to be—because of my brother. And I wanted to see the animals on my own. Think my own thoughts without worrying who was upset or who might possibly have a meltdown if one little thing went wrong.

"Don't be long, though, okay? Dinner will be ready soon."

"Okay. I'll be quick." Then I went back to my room, slipped on my shoes, and ran out the door.

The early evening sun had dipped low enough to cast shade over the road, and though it was still hot, it made the walk a little better than the one Jacob and I had taken earlier.

I read a little bit as I walked, and as I got closer, I saw the Not Open to the Public sign on the front gate of the zoo. I knew they'd eventually take it down and open the gate once everything was ready. But I wanted it to be open now. I needed to see that ostrich again. For myself.

I pulled out my package of Starburst and unwrapped one of the square fruity candies. They were kind of soft from being in my pocket.

Everything was quiet; the staff must have already left for the day. I couldn't see any of the animals from where I stood behind the gate, but I knew they were in there, resting and settling into their new homes. Did they like the space? Did they know they were somewhere different? Did they feel lost?

The sign glared at me and I glared back.

"Oh, come *on*." I pulled on the gate to see what would happen. It was held to the fence with a lock and chain, but the opening was just wide enough for me to squeeze through the gap.

Getting in wouldn't be hard, but I'd be in so much trouble if I got caught. So, I wouldn't touch anything, I wouldn't bother anyone, I wouldn't even stay more than a few minutes. No one would ever know I'd been there. I'd slip right back out and head home for dinner.

I pushed myself through the gap, tearing a hole in my T-shirt along the way, but I was in. I just needed to see the ostrich, and then I would leave. I wanted to see it without Jacob melting down beside me, crying and wailing. I wanted to see it in the quiet. Safe and found.

I felt bad, guilty almost, for the ostrich, and all the other animals. They were all locked in cages so people could come and stare at them. I knew what it felt like to be stared at. It was mean and unfair. And there was something scary about zoos, too. There were wild animals just an arm's length away. If the cages weren't sturdy enough, the animals could get out, and people might get hurt. I had to be careful.

I tiptoed across the makeshift parking lot as best as I could, trying not to crunch loudly in the gravel.

The exhibits were laid out in a large half circle. The donkey and ostrich enclosures were next to each other on the far left and were bigger than most. Those animals needed more space to move around.

The monkeys were in a tall cylindrical cage just past the ostrich pen. It looked like there were eight or nine of them jumping around and hanging from various limbs of the tree inside. As soon as they saw me, they started making noise. Screeching and chattering. Not in an alarming way, but like they knew I was something out of the ordinary, something they should probably be talking about.

After the monkeys came the tortoise in a low-walled enclosure.

Then, the Komodo dragon. Its enclosure was fenced in on all sides, and across the roof, too. On the outside of the fence was also a thick rope separating its cage from the rest of the zoo for safety. I thought about what Jacob had said about the Komodo dragon being a pretty fast runner, overpowering its prey, and the stuff about venom. I wondered if they would put up signs telling zoo visitors about the animals and their natural habitats.

I felt a chill as I walked closer, even though it was still warm out. I rubbed the goose bumps that had sprung up on my arms and unwrapped another Starburst.

In addition to the animal enclosures, there were three buildings: one that had an OFFICE AND MAINTENANCE sign hanging above the door, a tiny one that looked almost like a concession stand with a TICKETS sign, and a bigger building without a sign that stood a little ways off.

That was it. That was Prue's portion of "The Tulsa Zoo Coming to You!" It wasn't very exciting.

I continued on past each exhibit, slowly, until finally, I reached the ostrich enclosure.

Ostriches are weird. They're birds, but they don't fly. Jacob was fascinated by ostriches and knew all about them. He told me that their wings are more like decorations or accessories, and they flap them at their sides when they run. Running is their specialty. Thanks to Jacob, I also knew that ostriches only have two toes and walk the way dinosaurs did. He made sure I knew that they have skinny, featherless necks, too, and perched high above them are tiny little heads with huge beaks and giant eyes shaded by extralong eyelashes.

As I stood there, the bird approached on the other side of the fence, watching me with those big eyes, bobbing its head this way and that. It looked exactly like Jacob's toy. Only a million times bigger.

Sweat trickled down my back, and my neck itched where a horsefly had bitten me. I stayed quiet and calm, careful not to make any sudden movements. I didn't want to frighten her. Or him. Maybe I could even help.

"You okay in there?" I spoke softly, gently. "I'm sorry about before. I hope my brother didn't scare you with all his crying. Sometimes he just—"

Suddenly I heard the creak of a door swinging open. When I turned toward the noise, I saw a tall figure walk down the steps of the office building and across the parking lot toward me. She was dressed in khaki pants and a crisp white shirt. She put her hands on her hips, and we stared at each other. My heart rocketed around in my chest. There was no point in running.

I'd been caught.

6

·············

In Trouble

"CAN I *HELP* you?"

Her voice was clipped and clear. She offered to "help," but I knew she meant something else. Something like, *What are you doing here? Didn't you see the sign?*

My stomach churned and my head buzzed a little. All my thoughts felt like bees racing around, trying to figure out what to do. How to get out. But I couldn't move.

"Um . . . I . . . um . . ." I couldn't speak, either.

"Do you know you're trespassing?"

My stomach went from churning to a sudden drop. Like I'd missed the last step on a staircase. I knew I wasn't supposed to be there. But I didn't realize I had committed a crime.

I shook my head, then nodded. Slowly.

The woman sighed and ran a hand through her hair. I'd seen that look on my mom's face before. It said, *What am I going to do with you?*

"I think you should come with me," the woman said. My

stomach fell all the way to my feet, and, because my voice had quit working, I followed her without another word.

She led me to the small office building that was a million degrees inside. The air conditioner grumbling tiredly in the window wasn't doing much.

When the woman turned around to face me, I noticed her shiny name tag pinned to a crisply ironed shirt.

Vera Winslow sighed and sat down. "What's your name?" she asked.

"Olivia Grant." At least I got my name out.

I sat in the chair across from Vera's desk, trying not to stare at her arms while she questioned me. But it was hard to look away from the tattoos that ran up her forearms and disappeared into her rolled-up shirtsleeves. They were beautiful in a brave kind of way. They almost made me wish I had some, too.

"How old are you, Olivia?"

"Eleven. I'm so sorry. I never meant to trespass, Ms. Winslow! "I-don't-actually-know-what-happened-I-just-had-to-see-the-ostrich-because-my-brother-lost-his-and-it-seemed-like-a-good-idea-but-maybe-it-wasn't-and-now-I'm-in-so-much-trouble . . ." My words were working again, only they were coming out too fast and all jumbled together.

Vera held up her hand.

"Eleven years old is old enough to know better," she said. "The sign is posted on the gate to keep people safe from the animals, and to keep the animals safe from people. Do you understand? Just because they are in cages doesn't make it okay to be reckless. People have climbed into zoo cages and been killed."

"I would *never* climb into a cage. I was just—"

Vera held up her hand again. "We have every intention of opening the zoo to the public so people can come and visit. Once everything is ready."

I looked down at my hands.

Vera sighed again and set down her pencil. "I will need to inform your parents of what happened."

I couldn't meet her eyes. What were my parents going to think? Mom would get that tired look in her eyes and Dad would be so disappointed. I'd probably be grounded. No way would they let me audition for *Peter Pan* now.

Tears burned the back of my eyes.

But Vera wasn't done. "This is a big deal, young lady. I need to think about whether or not I'm going to press charges."

I felt sick to my stomach. And a little dizzy.

"I'm sorry," I said again. I didn't know what else to say.

Then Vera told me to go home. It was late. The sun had started to dip below the tree line, but I couldn't make myself hurry.

I was a criminal.

·····

"Olivia!"

Dad's voice called out to meet me on the dusty road. It was almost dark, but I could see his shape. I'd said I wouldn't be long. I'd promised to be back for dinner. Of course they were worried.

"Are you okay? We expected you back—"

"I know—I'm sorry—I—" And then I started crying.

"What's the matter? Did something happen? Are you all right?"

I nodded, sobbing into Dad's chest. "I'm okay. I just got into some trouble."

"What? What kind of trouble?"

"The kind that happens when you sneak into a zoo that isn't open to the public and get caught."

Dad held me at arm's length. His face told me he wasn't sure he believed it.

"What in the world were you doing inside the zoo grounds? That's trespassing!"

I sniffed. "I know. That's why I'm in trouble with Vera Winslow."

"Who is Vera Winslow?"

"The manager. Or head zookeeper. Or whatever. She's in charge. She said she would have to talk to you and Mom about what happened. But she wanted to make sure you heard it from me first."

"Oh." Dad seemed to consider this for a minute, and then he nodded. "Well. Guess we better get home then. Your mom is very worried." He put his arm around me and kissed the top of my head. At least he wasn't mad. Not too mad, anyway. Stupid zoo. It had already caused more trouble than a cage full of monkeys, and it wasn't even open yet.

Mom was standing in the living room when we walked in. A look of relief ran across her face, but it was replaced by questions a split second later.

"Where have you been? I was so worried! What happened? Are you okay?" She was wearing her I-was-worried-and-upset-but-now-I'm-glad-you're-safe face and using her I-want-an-explanation voice.

I sat down on the couch and slumped into the cushions. Guilt is heavy.

"She's fine," Dad said, answering for me. "She just got into some trouble at the zoo."

"Trouble?" Mom's eyebrows arched, and I started crying again.

"I didn't mean to! I really didn't! The gate just opened a little, and I needed to see the ostrich. I didn't touch anything, and I promise I'll never do it again!"

Mom glanced at Dad. She didn't look happy. But before any of us could say more, the phone rang.

7

Responsibility Hours

VERA CALLED THEM Responsibility Hours. Mom and Dad called them A Good Lesson. Ten hours a week, for eight long weeks, I would be working at the zoo to make up for trespassing.

That's why on a perfect Wednesday morning in June—the sort of morning you dream about all winter when you're riding the bus home from school and freezing—instead of riding my bike, or looking for Jacob's ostrich, or swimming, or doing *anything* I'd planned, while Mom took Jacob to therapy, Dad and I walked to the zoo.

Vera met us at the main gate. Her shirtsleeves were rolled up to her elbows. I could tell Dad noticed her tattoos.

"Good morning, Olivia," she said. "Thank you for coming."

As if I had a choice.

She reached out her hand to my dad. "Vera Winslow," she said.

"Keith Grant. Thanks for giving Olivia the, um, opportunity to lend a hand here . . ." He trailed off.

"My pleasure," Vera said.

Dad gave my shoulder a squeeze as Vera led me through the gate and locked it behind me.

I was trapped.

"I believe you've already had an informal look around yourself," Vera said.

I could feel my face redden. I turned to wave bye to Dad, but he was already on his way. "Still, I think a proper tour is in order, yes?"

I nodded and followed after her, trying to match her long strides.

Vera introduced me to the animals and explained what I'd be doing while I was here. Mostly laying new bedding, helping to distribute food to the animals, and cleaning out pens. It was pretty gross, but it's not like I was expected, or even allowed, to do any of that stuff alone. I was really just helping out the rest of the staff. And I guess it could have been worse. At least Vera didn't press charges.

She introduced me to Phil first, a gruff old man who kept talking to himself and was exceptionally crabby. Apparently, he'd lost his spare set of keys to the zoo. Vera seemed pretty concerned and was ready to send everyone on a search, but Phil insisted he'd find them on his own. I wanted to offer to help, but it didn't seem like the right time, and Phil didn't seem like the kind of guy who liked help.

Then I met Bridget, who was doing an internship with the zoo, and Maggie, the woman who'd been there the day before when Jacob melted down about his missing ostrich. If Maggie recognized me, she didn't say anything.

After the tour and introductions, I spent the rest of my time helping Bridget. It was harder to be helpful than I realized. First, I accidentally tripped and knocked over a bucket when I was helping her scrub the monkey cage. A little while later, I spilled a pail of feed for the donkeys. Halfway through my morning of Responsibility Hours, Bridget asked me to quit being so helpful.

Instead, I ran and got things when Bridget needed them, and held open doors and gates when she had her arms full. She let me go into the cages with her, too, as long as I stayed out of the way. But I was scared. Every time a cage opened, all I could think about was one of the animals getting out and trampling me. Or eating me.

The donkeys made me extra nervous.

"Their names are Daisy, Gretchen, and Mo." Bridget spread out a bale of alfalfa. "Daisy is Gretchen's mom. Mo isn't related to the girls, and he's kind of a crabby old guy, so if you ever walk behind him, make sure he knows you're there, or he might decide to kick."

"Oh! Okay." I nodded, making the sounds at Mo like Bridget showed me, but I still jumped every time he moved around the enclosure.

After we finished with the donkeys, we moved on to the ostrich pen.

"Last, but not least, is Ethel," Bridget said. The bird was watching us with a curious, disapproving expression.

"Her name is Ethel?"

Bridget nodded. The bird shook her own head up and down as if in reply.

I nodded, too. It suited her perfectly.

When I got home later, Mom was sitting on the porch watching Jacob. He was in the front garden digging holes with a shovel.

"Hello, Olivia," he said. "I am planting."

"What are you planting?" I asked.

Jacob didn't answer. It looked like he was just digging holes.

"He said he's planting breathing room for worms," Mom said.

"So, like, air? He's planting air?"

Mom smiled. "Yes, I guess so."

I sat down next to her, and she squeezed my knee.

"So, how did things go?" she asked.

"It was fine," I said.

She raised an eyebrow. I wasn't telling the whole truth and she could tell.

"I mean, it wasn't exactly great. Monkey poop really, really stinks. But I guess it could have been worse . . ."

"Okay. Well, good to hear. Are you hungry?"

I nodded and Mom stood up. "Jacob!" she called. "Time to go inside for lunch."

Jacob stopped his digging and followed Mom into the house.

I changed into some clean clothes and washed up. By the time I finished, Jacob was on to a new project, sitting at the table with a pair of scissors, cutting up long pieces of string into very short, tiny pieces. Mom said it helped him focus—making things that were big in his head smaller somehow.

She slid a turkey sandwich with cucumbers across the table to me. She'd cut the crusts off Jacob's sandwich, and she had left the top off, too, so he could put them on himself. He liked making sure they were straight. But Jacob didn't touch his sandwich.

"Time for lunch, Jacob," Mom said gently. "What would you like to do with your string while you eat?" She always let him choose, because if she chose for him, Jacob would probably melt down. Jacob didn't say anything for a minute, and then he started to cry.

"I want to put them back together. Can you put them back together? Put them back together? Back together? Together . . ." He said "together" three more times, hiccupped, and then took a deep breath, letting it out slowly like he was taking charge of his words again.

Mom nodded. "Good job, Jacob."

"Together." Jacob finished his thought without letting it run away again. And then he wiped his eyes with the back of his hand, put the top on his sandwich, and started eating.

Back together. What would it take to put all those pieces of string back together? And why would you even want to? I stared at the pile on the table. A nest of snipped thread. Jacob was over them now. He wouldn't touch them again. Once he was done with a "project," he never went back to it. After lunch, Mom would sweep up the pieces of string and dump them in the trash. So many pieces. Gone forever. Lost.

I thought about all the places I'd already looked for Jacob's ostrich. Every room in the house. Every closet. The crawl space under the porch. The bookshelf in the living room. I'd even searched some places in town, places Jacob had visited and taken the toy along. But I'd obviously missed something. Maybe I hadn't looked hard enough. I needed to double my efforts and do a more thorough search now. And this time, I would find that ostrich.

"Olivia, are you all right?" Mom was watching me. She'd said something and I'd missed it. I nodded and finished the last of my milk.

"I'm fine. I was just thinking. Sorry, what did you say?"

She sat down across the table from me and folded her hands in front of her. "Your dad and I were talking last night." Her face was serious. "We decided that as long as you handle this first week at the zoo well, we will let you audition for *Peter Pan*."

I dropped my cucumber on the floor. "What? For real?!"

"For real!" Mom laughed.

"But I thought I was in trouble!"

"You *are* in trouble for trespassing at the zoo. And I hope the hours you're spending there help you understand why it's important to follow the rules. So, if you have a bad attitude, or spend all your time complaining about it, you won't be allowed to do the play." Her serious voice shifted. "But just because you do something you shouldn't doesn't mean we will never let you do anything you enjoy ever again."

"Thank you! Thank-you-thank-you-thank-you! I'll have the best attitude ever and I won't complain and I'll do everything they ask me to do at the zoo! I promise!" I couldn't stay in my chair a minute longer. I threw my arms around her. She hugged me tight.

"But I thought you said that things—extra things—were too hard . . . with . . . you know." I glanced at my brother. He opened his sandwich and straightened out the cucumbers again. My stomach was jumping around, full of wings.

"Well, yes. But I think there's a way we can make this work for all of us." Mom glanced at Jacob, who looked up and grinned. Happy, like he was part of a secret.

"Olivia, your dad and I think it would be good for your brother to audition, too."

"Jacob?" It didn't make sense. I stared at her face. She was serious. "But Jacob can't audition for a play!"

"Why not?" Her voice held the tiniest hint of warning.

I looked at Jacob. He was listening and confused. He started rocking in his chair—my words were making him upset.

"Why do you think Jacob can't audition?" Mom asked again.

"His therapist actually suggested that more social interaction might be good for him. This would give Jacob a chance to express himself, safely, somewhere unfamiliar. And if I need to be, I'll be there, too, Olivia. You are not responsible for your brother."

"*Peter Pan*, written by J. M. Barrie, a Scottish novelist and play-wright. It is about a boy who never grows up," Jacob said.

I took a few deep breaths and tried not to lose my temper. Mom just said I could audition. I didn't want to lose that chance. But this was supposed to be *my thing*. I wanted this. For *me*. Jacob had never needed extra social interaction before. Why now? He would melt down. I knew he would. I wanted to be Wendy without worrying about Jacob messing everything up.

"I'm not saying he has to be in the play, Olivia." Mom sounded like she was trying to reassure all of us. "I'm just suggesting he par-ticipate in the audition. For the experience."

I nodded once and glanced again at the pile of string Jacob had cut up. Making big things small. Easier to process. What big things did my brother even need to process? Everything was taken care of for him. Everyone thought of him first. If anyone needed a piece of string to cut into pieces, it was me.

8

·············

Auditions

ONE WEEK LATER, I sat in the front seat with Mom. Jacob sat in the back doing the hand motions to "The Itsy-Bitsy Spider," with all of the seat belts strapped around himself, as we drove to the Tulsa Performing Arts Center.

It was just over a half-hour drive from Prue. Prue was too small to have its own theater company, but Tulsa had more than one, and this summer, the Tulsa Performing Arts Center had called in a traveling theater company to run their kids' theater program.

By the time we found a parking spot, got out, and made our way into the building, my stomach was doing flips. My excitement had turned into something else. Because of Jacob. And because we were late.

Jacob's socks had been too itchy. Before we left, he'd had to try on three different pairs until he found some that were okay. I'd begged him to hurry. But Jacob wouldn't be hurried.

By the time we got inside the theater, every other kid and parent had already taken their places onstage or in the audience.

I wanted to run down the aisle and up onstage, but Mom's voice stopped me.

"Take Jacob with you." She was quiet but firm.

"Take Jacob with you," he echoed. I closed my eyes. This wasn't a good start. But up the stairs I went, with Jacob following behind me. He was talking to himself, and I felt my face heat up as all the kids watched us walk across the stage. It's one thing to be the center of attention because you want to be. That's part of the reason acting in a play is so awesome. But it's another thing when people watch you with eyes full of questions.

We joined about forty other kids standing in a giant circle that was taped off on the stage floor. Some looked like kindergartners, and there were other kids who looked like they were older than me. The stage was full of voices and nervous laughter. Every kid there wanted a part.

Jacob stood next to me, shifting his weight from one foot to the other, but I didn't look at him. Did he even want to be here? I snuck a tiny look at his face, and he grinned at me. What if he had a meltdown? Could that ruin my chances of getting a part?

"Are you okay?" I whispered.

"I am okay, Olivia," he said loudly. I looked down into the sea of chairs and met Mom's gaze. I was nervous. She smiled encouragingly. I tried to smile back, but it was hard.

Everything was hard with Jacob.

The girl on my left was slowly twisting her fingers in a fold of her shirt. And even though she was standing perfectly still and smiling, I realized she was nervous, too.

"Hi," she said, her voice quiet. "I'm Amelia." Her brown hair was tied neatly into a ponytail with a yellow ribbon. She looked just like the Wendy on the cover illustration of my copy of *Peter Pan*.

"Hi," I said. I tucked a wild curl behind my ear. "I'm Olivia."

"What part do you want?" Amelia asked. "I want to be Wendy, but I think every girl here wants to be Wendy. Do you want to be Wendy?" She talked fast and didn't wait for my answer. But my stomach sank. I did a quick count. Easily half of the kids in the circle were girls. Maybe more. And Amelia was probably right. I bet every girl there wanted to be Wendy. That was a lot of competition. I cleared my throat.

"It would be fun to be Wendy," I said. "I hope the best girl for the part gets picked."

She smiled a kind of half smile, like she couldn't decide if I was saying something nice or not. I was trying to be nice. But I wished I had thought to wear a ribbon in my hair.

All the kids quieted down as a man and a woman walked onstage and made their way to the center of the circle. Except for an occasional cough, the whole place was silent. Jacob swayed beside me, rocking from foot to foot.

"Ladies and gentlemen!" The woman threw up her hands and

pivoted slowly, making eye contact with every person in the circle. "Welcome to the Tulsa Performing Arts Center! I am Dorothy—"

"And I am Stephen!" the man chimed in. "And together we are the Ramshackle Traveling Children's Theater Company!" They clasped hands and bowed, deeply. Everyone clapped.

"Okay!" Stephen's voice echoed across the stage. He was very enthusiastic. "If you are here to audition for *Peter Pan*, then you're in the right place. If not, you can stay anyway. We are going to have a ton of fun."

Dorothy stepped forward. "Now, before we get started, does anyone here know how to sing 'Happy Birthday'?"

Everyone on the stage politely raised their hands or nodded. "You are such a quiet bunch! Let's try that again. Does anyone here know how to sing 'Happy Birthday'?" Dorothy held her hand to her ear, and this time we all shouted "YES!"

"Ahh—much better!" She raised her hands like a conductor and began to lead us in the song. "*Happy birthday to you—happy birthday to you—*" We all sang along while Stephen walked around the circle in front of us, his hand cupped to his ear, encouraging us to "Sing out—sing out!"

Jacob smiled happily beside me because he loved music. But Jacob never sang anymore. I looked for Mom in the audience. Did she know there would be singing? The flyer hadn't mentioned this was a musical.

We sang a couple more songs as a group, loudly and enthusiastically. Then Dorothy asked us to sing "Twinkle, Twinkle, Little Star" one at a time. The room got very quiet again as one by one, around the circle, we each sang the song. Every voice was different, some loud and confident, some quiet and nervous, some in key, some not. Each person took a turn, and all the while Stephen took notes on his clipboard.

He and Dorothy were looking for something. For someone. For lots of someones, really. Stephen had a list of names on that clipboard, the names of every character in the play, and he was looking for kids to match with those names. I wondered if he and Dorothy ever got nervous. Were they worried they wouldn't find the right kids for each part? Would there be room to cast us all?

Suddenly it was my turn to sing. I tried to forget about being nervous and let all my excitement rush back in. I could sing this song in my sleep because I used to sing it to Jacob all the time; it used to calm him down whenever he got upset. And he would sing it to me, too—before.

I took a deep breath and I sang.

"*Twinkle, twinkle, little star*—" I imagined a quiet night, full of stars, and my brother leaning in to listen. It felt strange singing this song in front of all these people. But I liked it. My voice echoed in the large, quiet auditorium and rang out around me as I continued the song. It sounded clear. And in tune.

When I finished, Stephen nodded at me, making notes on

his clipboard. Then he gestured for Jacob to go ahead and sing.

And just like that, all the fun drained out of everything. Jacob didn't sing "Twinkle, Twinkle, Little Star" anymore, or "Happy Birthday," or "Pop Goes the Weasel," or even the ABCs. But Stephen and Dorothy didn't know that. No one here knew that except Mom and me.

I glanced at my brother. He was staring across the stage toward the back of the auditorium. Physically, Jacob looked like every other thirteen-year-old boy in the room. But inside, Jacob was definitely not like every other thirteen-year-old boy there, and I was mad that Mom had let him come. Mad that he was there. Mad that every kid in the room was going to see what Jacob was and what he wasn't. I could feel my face getting hot. Because I knew if I didn't explain, and Stephen tried to make him sing, something bad would happen. I didn't know what, exactly, because you could never be sure. But something.

"Um—he doesn't sing," I said softly. And I took a deep breath. "He's—"

"He doesn't sing!" Jacob interrupted loudly, echoing my words. Stephen kind of jumped, a little startled, and I jumped, too. My palms felt clammy, and I looked at Stephen, trying to make him understand with my eyes. I was afraid to say anything else because I knew Jacob would repeat it.

"What's your name?" Stephen asked.

"His name is Jacob," I said quickly.

"His name is Jacob," said Jacob, copying me again.

"And you are . . . ?" Stephen turned to me.

"Olivia. I'm his sister."

"I'm his sister," Jacob echoed.

Somewhere onstage someone laughed, and I looked across the room for the kid who thought it was funny. I tried to catch Mom's eye, too, but she was focused on Jacob.

Stephen ignored the laughter.

"Thank you, Jacob," he said. "Olivia." He smiled at me, and his eyes told me he understood. And then he moved on to the next kid, who quickly burst into a rousing rendition of "Twinkle, Twinkle, Little Star."

After the singing was finished, Stephen and Dorothy asked us to pretend to be different parts. Pirates, Indians, mermaids, crocodiles, birds, and other kinds of wild animals. All the characters that were in the play. It was fun saying "Arrrrrrggg" and squawking. Even Jacob was enjoying himself, but the whole time I was distracted.

Then we were divided into different age groups. I watched Jacob and a bunch of older kids follow Stephen across the stage and down the stairs. Mom caught Stephen as he was heading down the aisle with the group, and I knew she was telling him something about my brother. Stephen nodded at whatever Mom was saying, glanced at Jacob before saying something to Mom, and then he left to catch up with his group. Mom saw me watching and gave me a little "It's all right" wave.

But it was never truly all right. It was always right on the edge of something else. Not something terrible—not necessarily—just something awkward and uncomfortable and embarrassing.

I turned away from Mom and followed Dorothy and the rest of my group.

9

Brave

BACKSTAGE, DOROTHY PASSED out a few different scenes.

"These are a few lines from the play that feature parts we're considering you all for," she explained. "Stephen is reading some lines with the older kids for other parts. Like the pirates, and Captain Hook, and Mr. and Mrs. Darling."

My group read parts for Peter's Lost Boys, and for the Indian princess and her tribe of warriors, and for John, Michael, Wendy, and even Peter. Peter's lines were fun. We each got to crow like a rooster.

When it was my turn to read for Wendy, I tried extra hard to say her lines as I imagined she might say them. But they were kind of boring, and I kept thinking about Jacob. Wondering if he was doing okay, and what the other kids must have thought.

After we finished in our different groups, we joined back up with Stephen and the older kids onstage, and Dorothy made sure she had everyone's names and telephone numbers listed correctly on her clipboard.

"Now, if I can have your attention for just one more minute, please," Dorothy said.

I stood next to Jacob. I wanted to ask him how his audition went, but he wasn't very good at whispering, so I didn't say anything. I didn't want anyone to laugh again.

"Thank you all for this afternoon. We truly wish we could cast all of you. But Stephen and I want you to know that even if you don't get a part today, that doesn't necessarily mean you're not cut out for the stage."

Dorothy's voice was kind, but I didn't like what she was saying. Though it was a relief to know that they weren't going to cast someone if they weren't totally right for the show. Like Jacob.

"It just means that in this particular play, your talents would not be showcased as well as they might be in a different production. So, if you don't hear from either myself or Stephen by the end of next week, don't be discouraged. Instead, watch for the next production we do here at the theater and try again. Okay? Thank you all so much."

We all nodded and said thank you back, and just like that, the audition was over.

As we began filing offstage, I wondered how many others were afraid of not being right for the parts they wanted to play. Jacob walked off the stage like nothing had happened. Measured. Careful. Steady steps. But mine were heavy. I wanted to stay. I was *supposed* to be a part of this. I knew it. But I knew something else, too: I had been distracted. Because of Jacob. I wasn't able to focus as well after he repeated what I'd said. After someone had laughed. Maybe Dorothy and Stephen had noticed. What if I'd messed this up?

The phone rang just as we got home, and my heart leapt into my throat. It could have been anyone, but I wanted it to be Dorothy or Stephen calling to offer me a part in the play.

It wasn't.

"Hello, Mrs. Mackenelli." Mom had on her nice neighbor voice. "Yes. Yes, we did just get home." She looked through the living room window across the street to where Mrs. Mackenelli was standing at her window, waving at us. Mom waved back. And then she was quiet for a minute while Mrs. Mackenelli talked on the other end of the line. I could hear her voice, tiny and far away through the phone. "Oh, I see," Mom said. "Yes. Hmm." She met my eyes, and I knew Mrs. Mackenelli had lost her glasses again. "Yes," Mom said sympathetically. "Yes, I'll send her right over."

I opened the front door. "Come get me if Stephen or Dorothy calls, okay?"

"I think it will take them a little while to make some decisions, but yes," Mom said, smiling, "I'll definitely come get you if they call."

"Okay, thanks!" I said.

"Okay, thanks!" echoed Jacob.

·····

Mrs. Mackenelli's glasses were so familiar to me now, they could have been mine. Wide, round tortoiseshell frames with thick glass.

She set down my usual cup of coffee. Orion leapt onto his chair to join us at the table. He was just that kind of cat. I'd learned the hard way that Orion didn't like to be touched. Or if he did, it had to be on his terms—only how and when he wanted. Orion and my brother were alike in that way.

It didn't take me long to find Mrs. Mackenelli's glasses. I'd been finding them so often for so long now, it was almost like a game. They didn't even bother trying to hide very hard. They'd fallen behind the couch, or maybe they'd been dragged there. I think Orion was responsible for half the times those glasses went missing.

"Thank you, dear!" Mrs. Mackenelli smiled and set her glasses on her nose, looking around the room like she was seeing everything in a new light.

"So, what have you been doing today, Olivia?"

"Well, I auditioned for a play today—that's where we were coming back from when you called."

"A play! Oh! I always wanted to be on the stage." Mrs. Mackenelli twirled her hand in the air and struck a pose from her chair. I laughed, and Orion just stared at us like we were obnoxious and disruptive. "What play?" she asked.

"*Peter Pan*," I said. "Do you know it?"

"Yes, of course, dear. The story about a boy who never grows up."

I nodded.

"I saw it on Broadway back in 1950, a very long time ago. It was glorious."

"Jacob auditioned, too," I said.

"Oh!" Mrs. Mackenelli set down her coffee. "And how do you feel about that?"

I shrugged. "It's not like anyone will actually give him a part."

"Really?" She sat across the table, watching me.

"No way! Because, you know. What if he melts down onstage?"

Mrs. Mackenelli nodded. "Yes. I suppose that could happen."

"It would ruin everything." I sighed. "Mom just wanted him to have the experience."

"That was very brave of her," Mrs. Mackenelli said.

Brave? That seemed like a strange thing to say. Like she had picked the wrong word by accident.

"So, who are you hoping to be?"

I grinned and drained my coffee cup. "Guess."

"Wendy!"

"Yes!" I laughed. "How did you know?"

"Well, Wendy is the girl who loves Peter Pan and his band of Lost Boys. And you are a girl who has the most uncanny ability to recover lost things. It seems fitting that you would want to be that girl onstage, too."

I let her words sink in for a minute. She didn't know I still couldn't find Jacob's ostrich. But even so. "I never thought about it like that."

We were both quiet. And then she changed the subject completely. "Olivia Dear, you help me so much, I would like to pay you for finding my glasses."

"What? No, that's okay. I don't mind, really." She had never paid me before, and she probably needed her money more than I did.

"Well, I want to," she said. "And I insist." There wasn't much I could say after that, so I just thanked her and took the money. Ten dollars. It seemed like a lot to pay someone just for finding a pair of missing glasses.

"Think of it this way," she said. "If I had to purchase a new pair of glasses every time I lost mine, it would be very expensive. You are actually saving me quite a bit of money."

That made me feel better. I smiled, gave Mrs. Mackenelli a hug goodbye, and headed across the yard to wait for Dorothy and Stephen's call.

10

....

Won't Stop

JACOB WAS SITTING on the porch step waiting for me to come back from Mrs. Mackenelli's.

"Olivia!" He called out to me from across the yard. "Olivia, it's time for you to play a board game with me!"

"Hey, Jacob. Maybe later, okay?"

I wanted to finish rereading my favorite passages from *Peter Pan*. But even if I had nothing else to do, the truth was I hated board games. I always lost, especially when playing against my brother. Or, if by some genius stroke of luck I did win, Jacob would have a meltdown because he couldn't stand to lose. It was just easier not to play at all.

"No, Olivia! No, you WILL PLAY WITH ME NOW!" he screamed at me. And rather than argue with him, I marched up the stairs and into the house.

"Moooomm! Jacob needs you!"

"Why is he screaming? What did you say to him, Olivia?"

What did I—?

"I didn't say anything! I just didn't want to play a game with him!" But Mom didn't hear me. She was already outside with Jacob.

Later that evening, I searched for my brother's ostrich. Since it wasn't under the porch, and I'd already searched the whole house in the months since he first lost it, it only made sense to try the shed next—even though Mom and Dad didn't like us to go in there.

It was filled with our bikes, garden tools, lawn mower, and other random heavy stuff. I hadn't been inside the shed in years, and I didn't think Jacob had, either. It seemed like an unlikely place for him to lose something, but I couldn't afford to overlook anything now.

I didn't realize how cluttered it was inside until I started looking. If I was going to do a really thorough search, I'd need to clear it out first.

The lawn mower was heavy and kind of awkward. I had to push and pull a lot before I managed to get it out. But once I got it out of the way, I moved our bikes onto the lawn, too. Then two rakes and a garden hoe. Two lawn sprinklers and about three hundred feet of hose, yard games, extra birdseed for the feeders, bike helmets, and the broken tire swing that used to hang from the big oak tree in front of the house. Next I pulled out three pairs of gardening gloves, a plastic Ziploc bag full of various smaller packages of flower seeds, rope, and a hedge trimmer. There was also a chunk of Astroturf. And finally, a spool of clothesline and a box of clothespins.

But no toy ostrich. I even got a broom and swept out all the corners and the nooks and crannies overhead, just in case.

Nothing. No trace anywhere. I was sweaty and exhausted, and suddenly struggling not to cry.

Just then the porch door opened, and Dad came outside.

"Olivia?" He stood there in the yard, surveying all the things that used to be inside the shed. "What are you doing?"

I didn't know what to say.

"Well, I just figured, I, uh, would try to help around the house a bit more. You know, to make up for trespassing at the zoo."

"I thought that was the point of you working there," Dad said.

"Yeah . . ." I cleared my throat. I couldn't tell him the truth. He might tell Mom what I was up to. And she had already made it clear that she wanted me to go easy on this kind of thing.

"Well, your mom and I have seen how hard you've been working," Dad said. "We're proud of your effort, and your attitude has been great. Why don't you come inside for a bit."

"Okay." But it didn't feel like I was doing enough. And I wasn't going to stop until I found Jacob's ostrich.

11

....

Escapee

IT WAS THE middle of the night. The house was quiet. Except for the usual night sounds—the hall clock ticking loudly in the dark and the dehumidifier running in the basement—there was nothing out of the ordinary. But I sat up in bed, blinking and listening until the sound of my own breathing clouded the silence. The moon was unusually bright. And something seemed strange. I looked around my room for anything unusual, but everything was exactly the same as when I'd fallen asleep. I glanced outside, and then a shiver ran down my spine. I thought I saw something—*odd*. I went to the window and peered out, squinting, trying to make my eyes focus. It took a few minutes before my brain understood what I was seeing.

There was an ostrich in the backyard.

The giant bird was walking around, quietly. Step by step across the yard, just like a deer might. She even bent her long neck and occasionally pecked at the ground, like a deer nibbling grass. How had she escaped from her pen? Had any of the other animals gotten out? Where was the Komodo dragon? I knew that ostriches couldn't fly. But maybe they could jump? And how was she going to get back in her cage? Someone was going to have to catch her and bring her back, if she didn't run away first.

I leaned on the windowsill and watched her for a minute. How had she found her way to my backyard in the first place? If she was still here in the morning, I'd be in big trouble with Mom and Dad, and the zoo, too. And if she wasn't here, then what? Would she be safe out in the world when she was only used to living in a cage?

I had to do something. I crept down into the kitchen. The clock on the microwave read 4:37 a.m. I knew I should wake Mom and Dad and tell them, but something inside me didn't want to. I was the one who worked at the zoo, so this felt like my responsibility. And Mom and Dad thought I needed to be more responsible, right? Plus, I was a Finder of Lost Things, and this bird had lost her way.

I took a breath and let it out slowly.

If I was ever going to get close enough to catch her, I had to find something to lure her with first. I knew what ostriches ate now, because that's what happens when you work at a zoo. But I didn't have any ostrich feed. I didn't even have any birdseed. I looked around the kitchen. Granola. That was the closest thing I could think of. I grabbed the box. It felt light—almost empty. I opened it and saw we had just a handful left. It wouldn't be enough for the whole walk. So, I grabbed a box of Cap'n Crunch, unlocked the sliding glass patio door that led into the backyard, grabbed a hoodie and sneakers, and stepped outside.

Ethel was standing there in the moonlight. She turned her head, stretching her neck and kind of ducking back and forth like she was trying to get a good look at me, just like she had when I first stood in front of her cage. Maybe she recognized me. I shook the box of cereal, quietly, and made kissing noises, the way you call a dog. Her wing feathers ruffled as she kind of shook them out. Like she was thinking.

"Here girl," I called softly. "Come here. Don't be afraid. I've got something for you!" I was trying to be brave, but my voice shook. Scared-excited. Dad would be up around six o'clock, so I didn't have that much time. But still the ostrich didn't move. So, one step at a time, I inched across the yard in the moonlight, shaking my box of Cap'n Crunch and making friendly, encouraging "here girl" noises. I could feel my sneakers getting soaked in the heavy dew.

Ethel didn't run away, but she didn't come closer, either. She just stood there, looking at me with her big, big eyes. She blinked, holding very still, and I blinked back from just a few feet away. I wasn't sure what to do now that I was this close. I was afraid to touch her.

I opened the box of cereal and sprinkled some into the grass.

"There you go. You hungry, girl?"

The ostrich ducked her head, listening to the sound of my

voice, and then abruptly stretched her long neck and pecked up the cereal. I took a step or two back and sprinkled a little more in the grass. She took a step, too, and ate more cereal. Step by step, I led the ostrich across my backyard and down the road back toward the zoo.

The box of Cap'n Crunch was almost gone by the time we got there. It took me way longer to get Ethel back than I'd thought it would. The sky was starting to shift colors by the time I looked up and saw the zoo gate and its NOT OPEN TO THE PUBLIC sign. It was open, though, just enough for an ostrich to get out. I pushed the gate open a little more, and Ethel followed me back inside. But I couldn't bring her all the way back to her enclosure. I didn't want to risk attracting the monkeys' attention, or worse, get in trouble for trespassing again. Especially with Ethel out of her cage. What if someone thought I'd let her out?

I emptied the last of the Cap'n Crunch on the ground. "There you go, girl. Someone will be here soon to let you back into your cage." And while she was busy with the cereal, I sneaked back out of the gate and closed it tightly behind me, securing the latch. The chain and padlock that were usually around the gate were just hanging there. I wrapped the chain back around the gate and its post, and clicked the padlock into place. Vera would never forget to lock the gate, but maybe someone else had forgotten when they'd gone home the night before. Maybe I could find a way to casually ask about it when I came back soon for my Responsibility Hours.

·····

The sky was getting lighter and lighter as I ran all the way back home. I crossed through the backyard and through the patio door just in time to meet Dad on his way into the kitchen.

"Olivia! You're up early. What were you doing outside?"

I glanced down at my soaking-wet shoes.

"I, um, was just out watching the sunrise." It wasn't exactly a lie. I did watch the sunrise. All the way back home from the zoo.

"The sunrise?" Dad opened a can of ground coffee, and the smell of Folgers drifted into the kitchen.

"Yeah, I woke up early and it was really pretty." Again, not a lie.

"Okay. Well . . . good." He sounded confused, but I couldn't tell him I'd been bringing an ostrich back to the zoo for the past hour and a half. I'd be in so much trouble, and I'd had enough of that lately. Besides, if the whole point of my time at the zoo was to learn responsibility, taking Ethel back on my own was the responsible thing to do. It made sense to just keep quiet about it.

"You hungry? Want some breakfast?" Dad asked.

I was *starving*.

"I think your mom got some new cereal the other day . . ." Dad rummaged around in the pantry.

"Yeah, she did." I cleared my throat. "But it's gone."

He poked his head out of the pantry. "The whole box?"

"Yeah."

"Wow. You and your brother polished that off pretty quickly."

"Sorry," I said.

"Well, how about eggs then?"

I nodded, watching as Dad poured himself a cup of coffee and pulled a carton of eggs from the fridge.

When I arrived at the zoo later, everything seemed normal. Ethel was no longer roaming around by the front gate, and Vera was waiting to give me my assignments. I was dying to ask her about what had happened with Ethel, but then I'd have to explain how I knew she'd been out to begin with. Instead, I pulled on my rubber boots, found a wheelbarrow in the big storage building, and loaded up the tools I would need to help Phil with the monkey cage.

But first, I had to see Ethel. Just for a minute. So, I took a slight detour on my way to meet Phil. I needed to make sure Ethel was okay, and I wanted to see if she would be friendly after the morning we'd had together.

She wasn't.

She was just as disapproving as she'd been when I saw her in her cage the day before. It was like nothing had ever happened.

"Did you hear she got out of her pen last night?" Phil walked over to where I stood, staring at Ethel.

"Really?" I tried to act surprised. "Weird. Has that ever happened before?"

"Nope. First time."

"Did you put her back in her cage?"

"Yep. I did."

"Was her enclosure unlocked?"

"Yep. It was."

Phil didn't like to use any more words than necessary.

"So, someone let her out?"

Phil shrugged. "Guess so."

"Who do you think would do that?"

"Don't know," he said.

"Well, maybe someone thought she needed to go for a walk." I laughed a little, trying to be funny.

Phil glanced at me and raised an eyebrow.

"Never mind," I said.

"Let's go," he said. "The monkeys are waiting." Then he picked up my wheelbarrow and pushed it toward the monkey cages.

Phil didn't think things were funny. And he wasn't much for conversation. It's hard to talk to someone who doesn't want to talk back. But I was relieved he didn't seem to suspect I had anything to do with Ethel getting out.

Still, all the unanswered questions dug at my mind the way things do when something goes missing and I can't find it right away. Whoever had let the ostrich out was a mystery. If I paid attention and looked out for clues, maybe I could solve it.

12

....

The Pink Ones

BY THE END of the week, the zoo was ready to open, and I was starting to get the hang of things. I hadn't knocked over any buckets or spilled any bins of feed since my first day. None of the donkeys had kicked me, and even Phil didn't seem to mind when I was around. Plus, it was a great distraction from waiting for Dorothy and Stephen's call.

After I finished my hours on Friday, I stood in front of the ostrich enclosure. This had become our routine. The giant bird would walk around a little bit and peck at the ground a few times to see if I was really going to stay, and once she was sure about me, we'd just stand there and stare at each other.

I liked to imagine all the places she'd been before she ended up here in Prue's piece of the Tulsa Zoo. Especially now that I knew she had been out of her pen.

That afternoon, Ethel and I were staring at each other when a voice I hadn't heard before interrupted.

"I like the pink ones best," he said, inhaling deeply.

I jumped because I hadn't heard anyone walk up, but there

he was, standing just behind me wearing a white T-shirt, dark sun-glasses, and a grin. I glanced down at the package of candy in my hand. I was sucking on an orange Starburst, but I liked the pink ones best, too.

"Sometimes you have to eat through a lot of yellow ones, though. Before you get any pink. Do you think they plan it that way? I mean, imagine getting a whole package of pink ones!" He paused, thinking about that, and then shrugged. "Maybe they wouldn't taste as good, though, you know? Maybe it's the yellow ones that make the pink taste so good." He nodded, agreeing with himself, and then stuck out his hand in my general direction. "Hi. I'm Charlie."

"Oh," I said. "Hi. I'm Olivia. I work here." It felt good to say that to this boy in his T-shirt and shades. I shook his hand.

"Yes, I know," he said. "My mom told me about you."

"Really? Who's your mom?"

"Vera Winslow."

I blinked. "Oh," I said again. I had not been expecting that.

"She said I had to wait till you were more comfortable here before I could come and introduce myself."

"She did?"

He nodded and I stood up a little taller.

"Well," I said, "it's nice to meet you, Charlie Winslow. You want a Starburst?"

He grinned. I looked down at my hand, and then I grinned, too, because the next one in the package was pink.

By the time we were on our second Starbursts, I'd learned that Charlie and his mom lived in Tulsa, but that they were here in Prue with the zoo until renovations were complete. For the rest of the summer, basically. He was twelve years old, and he'd been around the zoo his whole life. He didn't have a dad. He liked radio talk shows. And he was blind.

I don't think I would have noticed that last part if he hadn't said anything. At least not right away. I mean, he didn't look blind. Sure, he was wearing sunglasses, but it was also sunny.

"How did you know I was eating Starbursts if you can't, um, see?" I asked.

He smiled and tapped his nose.

"So, you have like, super smell or something?"

"No," he laughed. "They just have their own smell and it's really fruity. Haven't you ever noticed?"

I sniffed the package in my hand, trying to remember, but I couldn't. I guess since I always saw things first, I didn't pay as much attention to what they smelled like.

And even though I didn't know all that much about Charlie, he seemed like the kind of person I could tell things to. Like whatever I told him, he'd keep it safe. So, I decided to let him in on my little secret.

"Ethel got out of her pen last night," I said in a low voice. "And out of the zoo, all the way to my backyard."

"What? She got out?"

I nodded. "Promise not to tell anyone?"

"We have to tell someone. It's important!"

"No! Please. I don't want to get in trouble. And I want to figure it out."

"What's to figure out?"

"How she got out of her enclosure."

"Why does that matter?"

"Because," I said.

"Can't you just ask Phil or Bridget or Maggie if the gate was left open?"

"I already know it was left open."

"Did *you* leave it open?"

"No, of course not! I don't even have a key. See? *That's* why I can't ask too many questions! I'm in enough trouble already, and people might think *I* let her out. I haven't been here very long; no one has any reason to trust me. The only reason I'm here at all is that I got caught doing something I shouldn't."

"You mean sneaking into the zoo?"

I felt my cheeks go red. "You know about that?"

He shrugged. "My mom told me. I think it's kind of awesome, actually."

"It's not awesome! It was stupid."

"But now you're here."

"Yeah," I sighed.

"Well, I'm glad." He grinned. "And I promise not to tell anyone about Ethel. For now, anyway. Maybe I can even help you figure out how she's escaping."

"Thanks," I said.

"Good thing it's just her and not one of the other animals. At least Ethel's not dangerous or anything."

"She's not?"

"Not really. I mean, not unless she gets scared or something. She was part of a petting zoo exhibit in Tulsa."

"Oh. Well, that's good to know. So . . . you really want to help me figure this out?"

"Sure." He shrugged. "I can be like your inside guy, gathering intel."

I laughed.

"And . . . you don't mind?" Charlie was suddenly nervous. He fidgeted.

"Mind? About what?"

"That I'm blind?" His voice had gone small.

"No. Of course I don't mind," I said.

Charlie nodded, and a wide grin spread across his face. It felt like we were agreeing to something important. I smiled, too.

13

....

Enough of What We Need

FRIDAY CAME AND went. It had been over a week since the auditions and still no call from Dorothy or Stephen.

Then Saturday.

I'd quit jumping every time the phone rang because Mom's phone rang too often to keep that up. But inside I was still asking, still hoping they had just needed more time to make their decisions.

We were eating breakfast Sunday morning when Mom's phone rang again. This time when she answered, I could tell it was them. I knew because Mom looked at me across the kitchen table and smiled, and changed her telephone voice from *Who is this?* to *So glad to hear from you!*

My stomach flip-flopped and I put down my toast. I tried to hear what they were saying on the other end of the line—tried to catch the name of the character I'd get to play, but I couldn't make out what they were saying. And then Mom's voice changed again, and she got up from the table. But I saw her glance at Dad before walking into the next room. It was weird. I looked at Dad, but he was wearing a look that wouldn't tell me anything. On purpose.

Maybe they were calling to explain why I didn't get a part? My stomach sank.

"*Olivia, I'm afraid you didn't get the part of Wendy.*" Or, "*Olivia, you get to be in the play, but you'll just be part of the general cast—you won't have any lines.*" Or, "*Olivia, they thought you would make a good tree.*"

But my mom didn't say any of those things when she got off the phone. Instead she called Dad into the next room, too, and that was *really* weird. I suddenly wanted to scream, or run around in circles. Instead I took a few deep breaths and clenched and un-clenched my hands in my lap.

The whole time Jacob sat beside me, lining up pieces of his cereal in neat rows across the table. He was making a pattern. A pyramid. Eighteen pieces of cereal on the bottom, then seventeen on top of that. Then sixteen. Fifteen. Fourteen. Thirteen. He was mumbling numbers as he went.

"One. Thirteen. Seventy-eight. Two hundred eighty-six. Seven hundred fifteen. One thousand two hundred eighty-seven. One thousand seven hundred sixteen." And then he went back down in the same order. When he got back down to "one," he finished with "Pascal's Triangle!" And then added another row. "One. Twelve. Sixty-six . . ."

Jacob knew things I would probably never know. And I really didn't care about knowing them. He did things I would probably never understand, too. Like making Pascal's Triangle, whatever that was, out of cereal on the kitchen table. But he couldn't make a phone call or have a normal conversation without help because he would say something weird or just set the phone down and leave the person on the other end wondering what happened. He couldn't go out to a restaurant without getting upset, or take a shower without having someone turn the water on and off for him. And sometimes, it made me angry. Because it wasn't fair. It wasn't fair that some people got to be normal and other people didn't. It wasn't fair that some families could just go places and do stuff without someone screaming and crying and melting down over the carpet pattern or the number of chairs at a table.

Dad said fair had nothing to do with it.

We'd just finished dinner one night; Mom and Dad had made me eat my vegetables. Every last one. But Jacob didn't have to.

"Fair isn't about two people getting or having the same thing, Olivia. Fair is about two people getting enough of what they need, when they need it," Dad said.

I needed this play now. I just hoped Mom and Dad—and Dorothy and Stephen—would agree.

"Olivia, can you come here a minute?" Dad's voice startled me, and I jumped up so fast that some of Jacob's pieces of cereal scattered onto the floor. We looked at each other for just a second, and then my brother started moaning. I crawled under the table, frantically searching for the pieces that had fallen.

"It's okay, Jacob! I'm so sorry. I didn't mean to ruin your pattern!" I was gathering bits of cereal off the floor like they were pieces of gold, setting them back on the table and trying to calm Jacob down as fast as I could because I was dying to hear what Mom and Dad had to say. "Shhh. It's okay, Jacob! I'll help you fix it!" But my brother only wailed louder and louder. And then with one swift sweep of his arm, he pushed the rest of the cereal off the table and sent it flying all over the kitchen.

"What is going on in here?" Mom came in looking frustrated, and Dad was right behind her.

"Olivia ruined Pascal's Triangle!" Jacob screamed, pointing at me.

"It was an accident!" I stood up. "I bumped the table and some of his cereal fell on the floor! I didn't mean to. Really."

Mom's face went from frustrated to sad, and a lump rose in my throat. What if they'd been about to tell me I had gotten a part in the play, but now they had to rethink whether or not I could do it? What if now they had to tell me no because everything—even breakfast—was just too hard?

Suddenly I couldn't hold them back. Tears started running down my face.

"Okay, okay, everyone. Let's just take a deep breath." Dad grabbed a broom and started sweeping up cereal. "Jacob, time for some more counting. Let's count Pascal's Triangle together." Dad looked at Mom with question marks all over his face, and Mom looked at Dad the same way. I almost laughed in the middle of my tears because they clearly didn't know what Pascal's Triangle was, either. "You start, Jacob," Dad suggested. And Jacob did.

Sometimes people think being autistic is about being smart in a special way, or having some kind of quirk that makes it hard to be with normal people because you're so brilliant. And that can be true. But other times, it's more like having cereal all over the kitchen floor, and melting down over Pascal's Triangle, and needing to have a big cry.

By the time Jacob calmed down, and Dad swept the kitchen, and I'd quit crying, some of the excitement about Dorothy and Stephen's call had faded. But not completely.

"So," Mom began, "why don't you come with us into the living room, Olivia." Jacob stayed where he was at the kitchen table, counting and recounting his cereal.

Mom, Dad, and I sat down on the couch.

"Before all of . . . that," Mom gestured toward the kitchen, "Dad and I were talking about the play and what part you got."

The butterflies in my stomach forgot all about cereal on the kitchen floor and jumped into action with a simultaneous loop the loop.

"I got a part? I get to be in the play? What part did I get?!" I couldn't stop smiling.

Dad grinned, rubbing his hands together and building the suspense.

"Are you sure you're ready for this kind of news?" he said.

"I'm ready!"

"Are you really, really ready?"

"Dad. I'm ready! Just tell me!"

Mom looked at Dad, and Dad looked at Mom, and they said it in unison:

"Peter Pan!"

What?

I looked at Dad's face first and then at Mom's, and then back again while my stomach went from excited to kind of twisty. Peter Pan was a boy's part. Dorothy and Stephen thought I'd be better at a boy's part than at being Wendy? It didn't make sense. I didn't want to be Peter. I wanted to be *Wendy*. I wanted to help lost people, like Peter Pan and his Lost Boys, just like Mrs. Mackenelli had said. I took a deep breath and let it out slowly.

"Oh, honey!" Mom said. "Are you disappointed? I get it, Olivia. It's not quite what you were expecting. Right?"

I nodded. I couldn't believe it.

"What part were you hoping for?"

"Wendy," I said. But it came out sounding more like "Windy" because my voice got stuck on the lump in my throat. I needed a minute to get used to this.

"Oh, sweetheart. It's okay!" Mom wrapped her arms around me. I could see Dad looking at her above my head. They were doing that thing where adults talk with their eyes.

"You don't have to accept the role if you don't want to," Dad said. "You could simply thank them and let them know you were hoping for a different part and—"

"Are you kidding me?" I looked at my parents. "This is amazing!"

My heart was racing. Can you explode from feeling too many things at once?

"Peter is the lead role!" I said, and Mom nodded. This was so unexpected. But *so* exciting.

Dad did a little fist pump, and I laughed. My butterflies were back. "I want to do it. I really do. Please, *please* say I can do it?"

Dad nodded.

"Woohoo!" I shouted. Because they could have said no. They could have said it was going to be too difficult. With Jacob. But they were letting me do something extra.

Dad held up his hands. "There's one more thing." He was still smiling, but he looked more serious, too.

I stopped jumping around. "What?"

Mom smiled. "Jacob got a part in the play as well." Her voice was calm. Like she was saying something totally normal.

"*What?*" Disbelief tasted like sour milk in my mouth.

"Now hold up," Dad said. "Let us explain."

"Explain? You don't mean you're actually going to *let him*?"

"Olivia, this is coming from Dorothy and Stephen, so before you get too upset, please listen to what they had to say."

"Before *I* get upset? What about Jacob?" Had Mom and Dad already completely forgotten about Pascal's Triangle? "Dorothy and Stephen don't know how he—"

"They *do* know," Mom said. Her voice was firm. "They called yesterday to offer parts to both you and your brother. They really liked how you two interacted onstage." She cleared her throat. "We had a very lengthy conversation about Jacob. His behavior. His potential to disrupt performances. The chance that he would have a meltdown onstage. All of it. And they listened to everything I had to say. I was very clear. And when we finished talking, Stephen told me that, given everything I'd just told him, he needed to speak with Dorothy before they made a final decision. I told them that your father and I needed to talk as well and decide what would be best for Jacob, if indeed they chose to offer him the part of a Lost Boy. Which they did. Before, on the phone."

"So, you've known since *yesterday*? You've known all this time and you didn't say anything? And, and how can you even think this would be a good thing for Jacob? That's the stupidest thing I've ever heard!" I was tripping over my words, sputtering as I tried to get them out. Tears were streaming down my face.

"Olivia, don't you think your brother deserves the chance to try?"

"But they've never worked with Jacob! And you know him better than anyone! How can you think this is a good idea?" I was choking on my tears now. There was no way I could play the part of Peter or even a tree if my brother was in the play. I couldn't do it. I wouldn't.

"I know it seems like a big risk, honey, but Stephen assured us that if things get to be too much for Jacob, at any point, they will let us know. And I'll be sitting in on the first few rehearsals, so I'll be able to see for myself, or help, if Jacob needs it. If we think it's too much for him, we can pull him out of the show at any point."

"Of course it will be too much for him! He can't even eat cereal without melting down!"

"Okay. Olivia, I think you're overreacting just a little. You're right. We do know Jacob better than anyone. Even better than you. And we think this could be very good for him. We understand he could make a mistake or have a meltdown or be disruptive. But this is a great opportunity in a safe environment. And it would allow Jacob to explore his ability to communicate and interact with others in a really cool, new way."

"But what about me? What about my opportunity? I had to beg you to let me even try out for the play! And then when I get the biggest part in the whole thing, Jacob has to do it, too? Just so he can go and ruin everything!"

Jacob was rocking back and forth in his chair at the kitchen table.

Dad closed his eyes and took a deep breath, letting it out real slow.

"Look, I realize you didn't plan on doing this with your brother," he said. "But that doesn't give you the right to refuse him the opportunity to try. His participation doesn't change the fact that Dorothy and Stephen thought you were perfect for the biggest role in the whole production! And so do we!"

That's what he said, but it didn't feel like anyone was thinking about anything besides my brother.

"I can't play Peter now!" I screamed the words. Jacob was slapping his hands against the top of the kitchen table, upset.

"Jacob, honey, it's okay," Mom said.

He could hear me. He could hear all of us. But I didn't care.

Dad sat up taller and straighter on the couch. He was tired of being patient. So was Mom. But I wasn't finished.

"I can't have Jacob ruin the play in front of hundreds of people! I just can't," I said. "And what does *he* even think? Did you even ask Jacob if he wanted a part? Or are you just going to make him do it whether he wants to or not—just like you do with everything?"

"We did talk to Jacob, Olivia." Mom crossed her arms, and her voice was tight. "Like we do every time he has the opportunity to try something he has never done before. We talked yesterday after Stephen called the first time. And Jacob was very excited."

"Oh! So, you talked to Jacob but not me? You told Jacob he got a part but you didn't tell me? Why didn't you tell *me*?" Angry tears were running down my face. I couldn't breathe.

"Olivia! That's enough!" Dad was done. "We don't need to ask your permission. And we didn't keep anything from you. We waited to talk about this because we wanted to have something real to say. We needed to be able to make a decision about Jacob's involvement before we told you anything. But you know what? You don't have to play the part of Peter! You can just forget it, if this is how you feel. Stephen said he'd chosen understudies for all of the major roles. He can give the part to someone else. If that's your choice."

This was the most unfair thing I'd ever heard of, and I didn't know how to make them see it. See *me*. All they could see was Jacob.

All they ever saw was Jacob.

Mom stood up. "Olivia, we want to give both you and your brother the best opportunities we can," she said. "Jacob is autistic, and that makes things more complicated. But he isn't incapable or unable to do this. And it would be wrong for us to deny your brother the chance to do something he wants to do just because it makes you uncomfortable, or because there's a chance that he might not get it perfect. None of us get everything perfect. There's always a chance we'll make a mistake, or make people around us uncomfortable."

My eyes had dropped to the floor. I couldn't bring myself to look at my parents.

"And you never know," Mom said. "He could surprise you and

be absolutely amazing. Just as I'm confident that you will be amazing as Peter."

Then she went into the kitchen to soothe Jacob, who was howling now. And I knew that whatever happened, nothing about Jacob being in the play would turn out *absolutely amazing*.

But they weren't going to change their minds. They'd decided. Nothing I had to say was going to make any difference.

Dad and I sat in silence until Mom came back into the room.

My tears were dry. The butterflies were long gone.

"Sweetie," said Mom, "why don't you take some time and think—"

"If Jacob's doing it, then I'm not."

Dad shook his head and scrubbed his face with his hands. "Olivia, you got the part of Peter Pan!"

Mom cleared her throat and looked at Dad pointedly. He didn't say anything else. We were all quiet for a moment. Then Jacob started howling again.

Mom spoke first. "It's up to you, Olivia," she said. "But you'll need to call Stephen back and let him know you've decided to turn down the role."

"What? I'm not calling! *You* can call! Tell them my amazing brother will take the part of Peter instead of me. Tell them I warned them when he screws the whole thing up! And don't bother telling me I have to go to my room, because I'm already going!"

And I went. Stomping and crying again, pounding my fist on the wall. I couldn't even look at my brother, still sitting and wailing at the kitchen table, as I marched to my bedroom. His sounds followed me all the way down the hall until I slammed the door shut.

14

....

Being Peter

I SAT ON my bedroom floor and cried.

I was stuck. Trapped between the stuff I wanted and the stuff that worked for Jacob. It wasn't fair.

After an hour or so, I got up and went over to the window, wiping tears with the back of my hand. I needed some space. There was no Neverland for me to fly away to, but I could take a walk. Just to clear my head. I tore a piece of paper from the notebook on my desk and scribbled a note for Mom and Dad. *"I went for a walk. Be back soon."* I left it on my bed in case they came in to check on me. Then I slipped out my bedroom window.

Unfair. Unfair. Unfair. Unfair. I trudged down the minimal maintenance road, kicking every loose rock and blade of grass in my way. The word matched my steps and circled around in my brain until it started to sound like *fair-run fair-run fair-run fair.*

I wanted to be Peter Pan, and I wanted Jacob to sit quietly in the audience. Everyone watching would say, "Hey! Isn't that the girl with the weird brother? She's different—she's not like him. She's great!"

People watched us all the time. They watched Jacob melt down in the grocery store and at the library, at the park and in school. They watched as we arrived places and as we left. They listened to us using our calm, soothing voices. Now they would watch for a different reason. This was my chance to do something just for me. My chance to be amazing. All I wanted was for Mom and Dad to watch and listen and clap and notice me, too. If Jacob was in the play, he would fall apart and all everyone would notice was him. Just like usual.

I kicked a little pebble as hard as I could and sent it flying down the road.

"*Oowwow!*" The boy I'd just met the day before clutched himself in the chest like he'd been shot. I must have hit him with the rock! "What the heck, Olivia! Are you trying to kill me?"

"Oh my gosh, I'm sorry! Are you okay?"

Charlie's face was red and his sunglasses were dangling from one ear. The long white stick he was holding dropped to the ground and broke up into smaller pieces. I could see he was blinking fast like he was trying not to cry.

"I am so, so sorry! I didn't see you there! Are you okay?" I asked again.

He nodded, straightening up and rubbing his chest. "You didn't see me? What, are you blind, too?"

"No—" I laughed, but I could feel tears rising fast. "I was just upset and not thinking—"

"And kicking rocks at your friends—"

"It was an accident, I promise!"

"I know." He smiled a little ruefully and rubbed his chest again. "It's okay. I could tell you were upset. I'm fine." He readjusted his sunglasses and put them back on.

"You could tell I was upset?"

"Yeah. You were talking to yourself."

"Out loud?"

"How else do you think I knew it was you?"

"Oh," I said.

"Are you okay?" Charlie asked.

I took a breath. "Not really." More deep breaths. Then I started crying again.

Sometimes things just felt too hard. I knew they were hard for Charlie, too.

We stood there and I tried to calm down. Charlie put his hands in his pockets and then pulled them out again awkwardly.

"I know you're crying," he said. "But I can't see it, so we can pretend you're not, if you want." I smiled a little bit, through my tears.

Charlie wasn't like anyone else I knew. He could sense things without me having to tell him, and he didn't seem to mind when I got upset.

We both sat down in the dust. The cicadas were rasping their singsong noise overhead from the dogwood trees and scrub oak.

Tiny grasshoppers rattled around us in the dry grass, flying up like tiny birds whenever we moved.

"Sorry," I said after a few minutes. "I'm just having a bad day."

"It's okay. Everybody has those sometimes," Charlie said.

"Yeah. It's just—I was going to be Peter Pan." The words came out a little shaky, and I sniffled again. "But now I can't. Because of Jacob."

Charlie's face was a mixture of wonder and confusion. "Well, I don't know who Jacob is, but being Peter Pan sounds kinda awesome!"

"Jacob is my brother. He's autistic."

I stared at Charlie, waiting for the change in expression that usually came over people's faces when they found out Jacob was autistic. It was something I had tried to explain to my friends after Jacob was diagnosed, but it still made them uncomfortable—being around him. Jacob never did or said the right kinds of things. So, making and keeping friends had always been a little difficult. But Charlie was different. He just nodded.

"Because of that, things are hard sometimes," I said.

Charlie nodded again.

So, I continued. "I tried out for this play—*Peter Pan*—and I was excited because I really wanted to be Wendy. But then Mom and Dad decided Jacob should try out, too, even though they both know Jacob could melt down onstage and ruin everything. Anyway, we both tried out, and I just found out I got the part of Peter

Pan—not Wendy—which was a little surprising because I'm not a boy . . . obviously . . . but still, I was super excited, until Mom told me Jacob got a part, too. And now I can't be in the play at all, because of Jacob."

Charlie looked confused again. "But why not? Why can't you be Peter Pan?"

"Because Jacob will melt down onstage and ruin everything!"

"Why? What part did he get?"

"He's a Lost Boy."

"That sounds like a pretty small part."

"Not really, but that's not the point." It didn't matter what part he had. Jacob could still ruin everything even if he was only a tree. "He will ruin the whole thing, I know it!"

"But what if he doesn't?"

"He will."

"So, what happens, exactly? What does he do?"

"He cries and screams and sometimes falls down on the floor and has a kind of temper tantrum. Sometimes he hits people, or hurts himself, and he throws stuff."

"Oh." Neither one of us said anything for a minute. "Has he always been like that?" Charlie asked.

"As long as I can remember, yeah. But you don't have to worry. Autism isn't contagious, like a cold. It's something you're born with. It's written inside of you. Kind of like a secret code."

"Oh," Charlie said again.

"Yeah. It usually starts giving away clues when you're a baby trying to walk and talk and stuff. Jacob was diagnosed when he was little. But he hasn't always been this bad."

"So, like, it can get worse over time or something?"

"I think so. I mean, Jacob's always been autistic, but I can remember when he was different. He wasn't always so easily upset by everything. And his meltdowns used to be smaller. Less crazy and way less frequent and stuff."

"Did something happen that made it worse?"

This I knew for certain. "Yes. He lost his ostrich."

"His ostrich?" Charlie almost laughed but caught himself. "What do you mean?"

"It was this little plastic toy Jacob had, and he loved it. But it went missing seven months ago, and since then things have just been getting worse. I looked for it a lot at first; I'm really good at finding things that are lost. Usually. I've been looking more and more recently, and I know if I can find it and give it back to Jacob, it will help. But I can't find it. No matter how hard I look."

"You're good at finding things?"

"Yeah. My dad calls it my superpower."

"That's cool."

"It is. Except when you can't find stuff."

Charlie nodded like he understood. "So, what kind of stuff can you find?"

I ran through the list of stuff in my head. "I don't know, I guess I've probably found almost anything you can think of."

"Dogs and cats?"

"Yes."

"Comic books?"

"Sure."

"Allowance and mittens and homework?"

I laughed. "No one's ever asked me to find missing home-work before, but I've definitely found lost allowance and a miss-ing glove."

"Hmm." Charlie kept up his guessing game. "Have you ever found a goldfish?"

"A goldfish? Who loses a *goldfish*?"

"Okay, fine. What about eyesight?"

"Eyesight?" I stared at him for a minute. Was he serious? "Oh, um . . ."

"I'm kidding," Charlie said. He ran his hands through his hair and looked off into the distance, seeing nothing.

"Oh," I said again. I tried to laugh a little, but it wasn't funny.

"I lost it a while ago."

"I'm sorry."

"Thanks. Me, too. I was really little. It was a car accident."

"That must have been scary," I said.

Charlie nodded.

"Do you remember what it was like? To see? Do you miss it?"

Charlie didn't say anything. Instantly, I knew I shouldn't have asked him that. It wasn't something you asked blind people. "I'm sorry—I didn't—"

"No. It's okay," Charlie said. "People never ask. And then I never get to talk about it."

"Okay. Good." I breathed a sigh of relief.

"I remember what it was like to see, but it's hard to explain. I was so young, and I didn't have the words then that I have now."

"What do you mean?"

"Well, it's like trying to tell someone what the color gold is when they've never seen the color gold before. So I can tell you how things *felt*, but it's hard to explain what I really remember seeing."

I nodded.

"I see colors in my head different from you. I mean, I think I do," Charlie said. "Red feels warm and deep. Green is sharp like grass and the taste of peppermint and the smell of sage."

I closed my eyes and thought about colors, trying to see them with everything except my eyes. It was hard. Seeing, and all the memories of things I could see, were stuck inside me. I couldn't just not see them.

"What about pink?" I asked.

"Pink is fruity and soft and sweet, like Starburst."

I smiled. Charlie was so easy to talk to.

"So, you really think finding Jacob's toy ostrich will help?" he asked.

"Yeah," I said. "I do."

Charlie nodded. "Okay. Then let's do it."

"Let's do what?" I asked.

"Find Jacob's ostrich. Look, I know it might be tough," Charlie said, "but I'm actually pretty good at solving mysteries, and with your finding-lost-things superpower, I think we could do it, if we tried together."

"Charlie, I've looked everywhere for Jacob's ostrich. I can't find it. I don't have any actual superpowers—I'm just good at following clues, but there's nothing for me to follow here."

"Or maybe you've just been doing it wrong."

"What do you mean?"

"Well, it's still missing, isn't it?"

"Yeah."

"I listen to this radio program on Saturday mornings, *Locksher and Son*. It's a mystery case–cracking adventure program where this kid and his dad solve mysteries together. They always start by making a map. I know. It sounds dumb. Who even listens to radio programs, right? But try explaining your favorite cartoon to me and see if I don't make a funny face or something." That made me laugh.

Charlie turned to me and smiled. I caught sight of my reflection in his sunglasses.

"Can I ask you a question?"

"Sure," he said.

"Why do you wear sunglasses all the time? Is it so people can't see your eyes because they look a little different?" The words were out of my mouth before I could take them back or think about them. I was full of the wrong kinds of questions. But Charlie didn't seem to mind. He just nodded.

"If someone can see, the muscles in their eyes are working all the time," he explained. "Helping them focus on stuff and adjusting to light. Keeping them straight and, like, *awake*. Mine don't do any of that. That's why they look different. They're kind of still. It makes people uncomfortable. Probably the way people get around you when Jacob has a meltdown."

Charlie was right. But I didn't say anything.

"Anyway, I can hear it in their voices. People turn their heads away when they're talking to me. So, it's just better if I wear sunglasses most of the time."

"Well, your eyes don't make me uncomfortable," I said.

"I know." Charlie smiled. "I can tell—you don't turn your head away when you talk to me. Even when my glasses are dangling off my face."

I laughed, but my face suddenly felt a little hot.

"So, what do you think?" Charlie asked. "Should we try making a map and search for your brother's ostrich together, or is that dumb?"

"No!" I shook my head. "I don't think it's dumb at all. I think it's kinda brilliant, actually."

"Awesome!" He grinned.

I smiled back. "And thanks for sitting here. With me. Even though I almost killed you with a rock."

He laughed. "Yeah. You're a good shot! It's lucky I work out." He flexed and puffed out his chest before deflating like an inner tube. And then I knew for sure that even if I didn't have a super-power, Charlie did. He was an expert at making other people feel things. Better things. About themselves. He could have just sat around feeling bad about being blind, but he didn't. Charlie was try-ing his hardest to be himself, no matter what anyone else thought. He made me want to try, too.

I stood up and brushed the dust from my jeans.

"Do you want me to walk you back to the zoo?" I asked. He thought about it and nodded once. He and Vera were renting a trailer parked on the zoo grounds. I hadn't noticed it before be-cause it sat back behind the largest of the three buildings.

"Probably wouldn't be good to get lost out here and eaten by some wild animal," Charlie said. Then he started feeling around on the ground for something next to him. When he found what he was looking for, like magic, he shook it out until each piece snapped together. The same way the tent poles snap together on our camp-ing tent. He held it out so I could see. And I realized it had been a cane—not a stick—he was using when I first saw him on the road earlier.

"Whoa. Cool. You always keep that with you?" I asked.

"Yeah. It's like eyes for my ears and feet. Helps me feel the world around me." He gently tapped the cane on the ground. "I can hear and feel what's in front of me so I don't bump into anything or fall off a cliff."

"Right," I nodded. "Good thing you avoided those on your way here. So many cliffs in Prue."

He laughed.

"Why were you coming down the road all by yourself anyway?" I asked.

"You live around here," he said. "First house at the end of this road, right? Mom told me. So, I figured I'd just come find you and see what you were up to."

"Really? You were looking for me?"

"Yeah. Come on." Charlie had already started down the road, tapping his cane in front of him, throwing up little puffs of dust and scattering grasshoppers as he went. He walked pretty quickly for someone who couldn't see where he was going. He didn't need me, and there weren't any cliffs in Prue, Oklahoma. But I wanted to walk with him anyway. I hurried to match my steps to his.

"So, tomorrow works then, right?" I said. "After I finish at the zoo? We can start looking for Jacob's ostrich. The sooner we find it, the better."

"Sure, that sounds great!" Charlie said.

"Okay, good. We can come back to my house after I'm done working."

"Perfect." Charlie smiled and his cane *tap-tap-tapped* and *swish-swished* back and forth in front of us. "So, you're really gonna turn down Peter Pan?"

We were almost back to the zoo. Charlie broke apart his cane and stuffed it into his back pocket.

"Well . . ." I dug my toe into the dust. "I really want to be in the play. And I really, *really* want to be Peter Pan." I sighed and stuffed my hands in my pockets. "Plus, I doubt Jacob will even make it through rehearsals and stuff before everyone sees how he is and decides it's not a good idea."

Charlie was kind of frowning, but he nodded.

"And if he does make it all the way through rehearsals and gets to performances and then melts down onstage and ruins every-thing, well . . ."

". . . You'll still be able to tell people you can fly!"

"Yeah!" I smiled and tried to believe it would be that easy. "Yeah."

"Good," said Charlie, more serious. "I'm glad you're going to do it. And maybe Jacob will surprise you."

"Yeah right."

"Well, I still think you'll be great," Charlie said.

"You do?"

"Absolutely."

"Why?"

He shrugged. "Just a feeling."

And whatever feeling he had, his superpower was working, because after we said goodbye, I walked back down the minimal maintenance road almost like someone had sprinkled pixie dust on me. Almost like I could fly.

15

Decisions

WHEN I GOT back home, Mom and Dad were furious. Dad was walking back and forth across the kitchen, over and over. And then he leaned against the counter like he was too worked up to sit down, arms folded across his chest.

"Are you going to tell us where you were?" Mom asked.

"I—I went for a walk, like I said in my note. I went down the road toward the zoo, and met my friend Charlie Winslow about halfway there. He was taking a walk, too. We just sat and talked." I was definitely in trouble. Again. I knew when I wrote the note and slipped out my window that they'd worry. Maybe I had even wanted them to.

"Charlie Winslow? I've never heard you mention him before."

"I just met him yesterday, actually. He's Vera's son. He's very nice."

Mom leaned back in her chair, her forehead wrinkled. Dad just nodded slowly.

"Okay," he said. "Well, what kinds of stuff did you talk about?" He seemed more interested than upset all of a sudden.

"Just stuff. Autism. And the play," I said. "Things that go missing, and how I'm good at finding them. He's blind, so we talked about that, too. I told him about Jacob's ostrich. Stuff like that."

"Oh."

We were all quiet, and then Dad sighed and sat down heavily in a chair.

"Okay, Olivia. Here's the deal. You are not allowed to leave the house without telling us where you're going. Not ever. Or at least not until you are much older than you are now. Are we clear? Your mom and I were very worried."

"Sorry," I said softly.

"I can understand if you need to take a walk or if you need some time alone to think," Mom said. "I feel that way, too, sometimes. But you need to let us know where you're going. Even if you're upset. Even if *we* are upset. Is that clear?"

I nodded.

"And also, you need to call Dorothy and Stephen before it gets any later. They need to know what you've decided about the play."

I took a deep breath. Even though I didn't know what it would be like to be in a play with Jacob, this wasn't about him. It was about me. "Actually, I changed my mind," I said.

"You did?"

"Yes. I want to be Peter Pan. I really do. And even if Jacob has a meltdown and ruins the whole play, well, at least I'll be able to tell people *I can fly*." It sounded even better now than when Charlie had said it.

Dad smiled. "I'm glad to hear it, honey."

I didn't tell them why I had changed my mind. And I didn't tell them about my new plan to search for Jacob's missing ostrich, either. How if Charlie and I could just find the ostrich—before opening night—it wouldn't matter if Jacob was in the play, because he wouldn't melt down and he'd be able to go back to being the kind of person he was before he lost it.

I didn't say any of that. I just took the slip of paper with the phone number on it from Dad and called the Ramshackle Traveling Children's Theater Company. I listened as the phone rang once, twice, three times.

"Hello, this is Dorothy."

"Hello! This is Olivia Grant. I'm calling about the part you offered me in—"

"Olivia! I'm so glad to hear from you!" she said. "Have you called to tell me you're ready to be our Peter?"

I laughed. That sounded so good.

"Yes, I am!" I said. "I'm ready to be your Peter Pan."

16

....

Mapping It Out

I'D BARELY HUNG up the phone when Jacob suddenly wailed long and loud from where he was working on his puzzle in the living room. My smile fell to the floor. I watched seven hundred miniature puzzle pieces go flying as Jacob flipped over the card table he'd been working on.

"Jacob, what—?" Mom jumped up, and Dad heaved a small, weary sigh.

It didn't always take much, but if Jacob was tired or overexcited, or just a little too frustrated, a meltdown was almost certain.

Mom and Dad put their calm, determined faces on and went to work.

"It's okay, Jacob. Here, why don't we make a few small piles, okay?" Mom said. "Can you put all the blue pieces over here?"

"Great idea," said Dad. "I'll help you, Jacob."

But Jacob ignored them. He kicked the card table and fell to his knees in the middle of all the puzzle pieces.

"Nooooooooooo!" He screamed and rolled around. I inched

away until I was against the wall. Jacob just kept thrashing, and then he tried to bite Dad.

I froze. All I could do was watch. I was . . . afraid. I was afraid of my brother.

I'd never been afraid of him before.

"Ahhhhhhhhhhhhhh!" He yelled and thrashed around, throwing puzzle pieces like rocks on a playground.

I remembered what Mom had said—about Jacob needing to make big things small. Only, whatever was big in Jacob's head, he couldn't seem to get it into small enough pieces now. Or maybe there were too many pieces to start with, because when he finally did calm down, he just sat there in the middle of the living room floor, his knees pulled up to his chest, rocking back and forth.

Mom and Dad sat there with Jacob on the floor, their shoulders hunched and their faces tired. They didn't touch him because Jacob was showing us that he didn't want to be touched. It was awful.

I squeezed my arms tighter and tighter, too, trying to hold all the pieces of myself together.

Later that night, I lay in bed, listening to Mom and Dad in the kitchen. I knew I shouldn't eavesdrop, but I couldn't help it.

"He's getting worse."

"No, sweetheart, he's just tired tonight, and so are you . . ."

Dad's voice trailed off and they talked some more. I couldn't hear everything, but words like "therapy" and "treatment" kept coming up, and then I heard my mom say something that made me sit up in bed.

"I think it's time to have him reevaluated. Officially. I think his therapist will agree. I need to know that it's not something I'm imagining. And if he *is* getting worse, we need to look at options." She paused. "I'll call in the morning."

I couldn't hear much else after that, so I tried to go to sleep. But I couldn't.

The sound of my brother crying and screaming over those puzzle pieces echoed in my ears. And the way he had looked at us—but also, *not* looked at us—was seared into my brain. Like one part of him was crying for help and the other part of him didn't even know what was going on. He'd looked lost. I didn't even know it was possible to get lost like that, inside your own skin.

Hours later, I still couldn't sleep. I sat in bed and pulled my knees to my chest. I held myself together there, in the dark. I needed to fix this. I needed to find Jacob's ostrich.

Charlie said we should start with a map. But I couldn't wait for him. I needed to do this now. I climbed out of bed, switched on my desk lamp, and looked around for a piece of paper. All I could find was my little notebook, and that wasn't big enough. Mom had some paper on her desk. I opened my door and tiptoed out into the hall. I didn't want to wake anyone up.

"Hello, Olivia!"

"Eeeee!" I kind of half squeaked, half screamed. My brother jumped. He was standing in the middle of the living room, alone, in the dark.

"What are you doing out here, Jacob? You scared me!" I was whispering, but I wanted to be yelling.

"I am okay, Olivia," he said. "I am okay."

"Well, that's great," I whispered. "Why don't you go to bed, Jacob."

"Okay. Good night, Olivia," he said.

"Night."

I waited until he was in his room with the door closed before I snuck into Mom's home office and switched on the desk lamp.

I never meant to snoop. I was just looking for a piece of paper. But as I started opening drawers and shuffling through the things on Mom's desk, I saw it. An article. She was always reading about autism. Always trying to learn more so she could help Jacob. But this article was different.

Recurrence of Autism Spectrum Disorders in Siblings

I picked up the paper and held it. And then my hands started shaking so much I had to set it back on her desk. Why was she reading an article about the possibility of multiple kids in the same family being autistic? Did Mom think I could be autistic, too?

I was breathing fast. Too fast. I had to sit down.

My hair felt like it was lifting off the top of my head. Did she think I could be like Jacob? *No!* That was *impossible.* We were so different!

I stared at the words on the page in front of me, reading very slowly. Reading some things more than once. Trying to make sense of it all.

The article was about the likelihood of brothers or sisters of autistic kids being autistic, too—even if they don't show signs of it when they are little. It was called latent autism, which, according to the article, was another way of saying someone could start being autistic when they're older. Then it went on to say some stuff about technical genetic mutation that I didn't understand. Something about how certain genes could be tied or linked to parents and children and aunts and uncles and cousins. Not that autism was hereditary, exactly, but that genetic anomalies and mutations sometimes got passed along.

I set the paper back down on Mom's desk and took a deep breath. Was I dreaming? I shook my head a little and looked around the room, just to be sure. Everything seemed normal. It was dark, except for the light that flooded over Mom's desk. I could hear Dad snoring down the hall. Everything else was quiet. I was definitely awake.

I rested my head on my arms, taking deep, shaky breaths and trying not to cry. Why would Mom think I could be autistic? Did

Dad think so, too? Did I act like Jacob? Did I do the same kinds of things he did? What kinds of things were autistic things? I reviewed what I knew. Getting really upset over small things. Acting a whole lot younger than your age. Solving problems in strange or unique ways.

I tried to think back, and the longer I thought, the harder it was to breathe. Because there *were* things. I lost my temper too fast sometimes. I stomped my feet and slammed doors. I ran off down the road toward the zoo without telling anyone. I was extraordinarily good at finding things because of the way I could remember details and gather clues. I didn't have very many friends, but what if that wasn't because of Jacob? What if it was because of *me*?

I clapped my hands over my mouth, trying not to make a sound, but I felt like screaming. I shut my eyes and started counting instead, because it was the only thing I could think of. Mom counted with my brother sometimes, to help him focus and calm down. *1-2-3-4. Deep breath in. 1-2-3-4. Let it out. 1-2-3-4. Another deep breath. 1-2-3-4. Let it out again.* By the time I'd counted to four and breathed eight times, I could take my hands off my mouth. I was still shaking, but I had an idea.

I snatched a few pieces of paper from Mom's desk, tiptoed back down the hall to my room, and grabbed a notebook from my bedside table. I rummaged around in the drawer until I found a red pen.

After Jacob lost his ostrich, he started acting even more different. All the things that bothered him before began to bother him much more. All of his little tics got bigger, and he did them more often. Rocking, twisting his shirtsleeves, copying what people said—*Had he known that things were changing inside him?* I wondered.

I had an advantage. I knew that things could be changing inside me. And I knew what kinds of behaviors were autistic things. If I could keep myself from doing those things, I could keep myself from becoming like Jacob. The only hard part was that sometimes it was tough to determine what was an autistic behavior and what was an emotional behavior, where Jacob was just acting on what he felt. So, I had to be extra aware, and I had to keep myself in check.

I opened the notebook and wrote the date at the top. On the first page, I wrote *Olivia's Neverdo List*. I needed a way to keep track.

One by one, I carefully listed everything I had done that might be considered autistic, or even just overly emotional reactions. If it was on my list, it would be a reminder to never do it again—unless I wanted to be like Jacob.

1. Never overreact.
2. Never lose my temper.
3. Don't yell at Mom and Dad.

4. Don't stomp my feet, pound on wall, or slam doors.
5. Don't cry uncontrollably.
6. Never kick rocks and hurt people (even by accident).
7. Don't talk to myself out loud.

When I finished, I closed my notebook and made a promise to myself not to do any of those things tomorrow. I would work as hard as I could to be normal and calm. And in the meantime, I wouldn't stop searching until I found Jacob's ostrich.

I would fix this. For Jacob—and if I could fix it for Jacob, I could fix it for me, too.

Then I grabbed the pieces of paper I had taken from Mom's desk and smoothed them out. If I was going to make a map, I had to track down the details so I could make a calculated search of all the possible places Jacob could have lost his ostrich. I had to be smart about this, and I needed to look for new clues. Seven months was a lot of time for something to be missing. But timelines weren't as important as *places*, and I'd already searched many of them. So, that was a start. With this map, my ability to find missing things, and Charlie's help in clue gathering, we could do this.

Only now I had a new deadline. I had to find that ostrich—*now*. Because if Mom and I were right, and if Jacob was truly getting worse—if his autism was progressing or growing, or getting bigger—was there a point of no return? Could the old Jacob be lost forever?

I shivered.

If that was true for Jacob, then it was true for me, too. This felt like a race against time. And against myself.

I racked my brain, thinking, and then drew a picture of our house in the middle of the page. It was as good a starting point as any. Thank goodness we'd never moved! It wasn't perfect, but it looked pretty much like our house—if you were a giant and had lifted the roof off so you were looking at it from above. I marked the recent places I'd already looked for the ostrich with a small X—like the porch and the shed. That way I wouldn't waste time searching where I didn't need to. Maybe Charlie was right. Maybe this was the way real finding happened.

If I still couldn't find Jacob's ostrich after I searched the whole house again, I'd go back to the other places Jacob went, like the library, the park, and the grocery store—that kind of thing. On a second piece of paper, I drew those places, too, and then I taped both pages together.

It was going to be tricky, but it was so nice to know I wouldn't have to do everything on my own. That I'd have Charlie's help. I only hoped it would make a difference. Even if it didn't, it would be nice to have his company. To have a friend. I couldn't risk losing that. So, I couldn't tell Charlie about this new development—about the article I'd found. It would change everything.

Suddenly, I heard a slight rustle, and I looked up. There, in the backyard, was Ethel. A life-size version of my brother's ostrich. Real. And very much out of her enclosure. Again.

I pushed back the curtains. The giant bird caught the movement and froze in the yard, watching me.

Mom and Dad had forbidden me to leave the house without telling them where I was going. I thought about it for a minute and then tiptoed out of my room and down the hall, past the kitchen and living room, past Jacob's room, and to my parents' closed bedroom door. I opened it just a crack.

"Mom? Dad?" I whispered.

No answer.

"I promised to tell you if I was leaving the house. Well, I'm telling you. I'm leaving the house. I'm bringing Ethel back to the zoo."

No answer. Just Dad's snoring.

"Okay. I'll be back soon," I told them.

Just like I promised.

17

Guessing the Direction of the Wind

I WALKED ETHEL back to the zoo for the second time, leaving a trail of Cap'n Crunch for her to follow. And once she was inside the main gate, which was unlocked again, I raced home in the dark.

Running in the dark is dangerous because your imagination can convince you of pretty much anything. Even once I was back in my own house, in my own room, and snuggled under my covers, my heart wouldn't quit racing.

Finally, as the sky was beginning to lighten, I fell asleep.

I woke up with thoughts of Peter Pan racing around in my head. In the excitement of bringing Ethel back to the zoo last night, I'd forgotten that today, this very afternoon, I would climb the stairs to the stage and be Peter Pan for the first time. Or at least practice being him. Butterflies swirled around in my stomach. I pushed them down.

First, I had Responsibility Hours.

.....

Charlie came to greet me at the gate, his cane *tap-tap-tapping* in front of him, and let me inside the zoo.

"Ethel got out again!" he said.

"I know," I said, yawning.

Charlie's mouth fell partly open. "Did she get *all the way out?!* She was out of her enclosure here inside the zoo, but the main gate was locked this morning!"

"That's because I closed the padlock again once she was inside," I said. "I probably should have brought her all the way into her own enclosure, but I was afraid someone would see me."

Charlie let out a big breath.

I continued. "The chain and lock were just hanging on the fence, and the gate was wide open when we got here. Someone has to be letting her out. There's no other way Ethel could escape her own enclosure and the zoo's main gate. Right?"

Charlie nodded.

"What are we going to do?" I asked.

"I think we need to tell my mom, Olivia."

"No! Please. Please don't say anything, Charlie." I grabbed his hand, as though just by hanging on to it I could keep him from doing anything. "I'll be in so much trouble!"

"Why will you be in trouble? You're not the one letting her out. Are you?"

"No, but she's gotten out twice now, and both times she's ended up in my backyard. Who on earth is going to believe it isn't me?"

Charlie frowned a little and then sighed. "Okay. I won't say anything for now. But if we don't figure out how Ethel is getting out pretty soon, I'll have to tell my mom."

"I know," I said. "Okay. Thanks."

Charlie nodded.

"This is so crazy," I said.

"Yeah. I had no idea things would be this interesting in tiny Prue, Oklahoma! I was totally prepared to be bored out of my mind this summer."

"Well, things usually are pretty quiet around here."

"Then I hold you responsible," Charlie said. His whole face was smiling.

"I do try to take my responsibilities seriously," I said. I was smiling, too. "Oh! And I made a map! Like you suggested. So we can start searching for my brother's ostrich."

"Oh . . . okay." Charlie's smile faded a little.

"What's the matter?"

"I thought we were going to work on it together."

"We are!" I cleared my throat. "I just couldn't sleep last night. I wanted to get a head start on things."

"So, you still want my help?"

"Yes! Definitely."

"Okay. Awesome." Charlie's smile was back. "What does the map look like?"

"Well, I started with my house, right in the middle. And then

I drew other places that my brother has gone. Like the library, and the park. I'm hoping if we go and visit those places and I think about his ostrich really hard, I'll be able to remember some things, or notice details I might have missed before."

Charlie tilted his head like he was thinking about that.

"So, all you have to do is think about a missing thing and it, like, shows up or something?"

"No." I smiled. "But if I have a picture in my mind of the missing thing, and if I'm in the general place where that missing thing is, then clues become clearer somehow. I remember details—seeing something that reminds me of something else. Like this one time, I was looking for my dad's missing keys, and I remembered that he usually sets them in the bowl by the front door. So, I started wondering if maybe he'd been distracted and put them in a different bowl somewhere else in the house. Sure enough, I found them in the fruit bowl in the kitchen."

"Wow," Charlie said.

"It also helps if I know the person who's lost the thing I'm looking for. Like, I know my dad. Jacob is a little trickier because he's autistic. Some things he does exactly the same way every time. I mean, he still gets dressed as soon as he wakes up every morning, just like he's going to school, even though it's summer. But then, other times he will do something totally out of the ordinary. It's tough because he's a little more unpredictable."

Charlie nodded. "Okay. So, finding your brother's missing

ostrich will be as easy as being in the right place and remembering the right details, or as hard as guessing the direction of the wind next week?"

"Yeah," I laughed. "Basically."

Charlie shrugged nonchalantly. "We've totally got this."

When we got home later that afternoon, Mom was in her office. I could hear she was on the phone. Her voice was serious and my stomach knotted. Charlie and I stood in the hall, listening for a minute. She was talking about Jacob, about scheduling a reevaluation. Finding Jacob's ostrich suddenly felt even more impossible than guessing the direction of next week's wind.

I knocked on the door lightly to let Mom know I was there, and waved hello before Charlie and I headed into the kitchen. But I couldn't stop thinking about that article on Mom's desk. Did she really think I was like Jacob—or could be like him eventually? Did she see him every time she looked at me? I swallowed, suddenly trying not to cry, and I stared at the pictures on the refrigerator. Pictures of family. Old holiday photo cards of friends. Lists of things Mom didn't want to forget or things she needed to do. Magnets with quotes on them. "Coffee runs this house." "Smile, happiness looks good on you." "Do it today. Someday never comes."

"Is everything okay?" Charlie's voice sounded a little nervous, and I smiled and nodded before remembering he couldn't see me do either.

"Yeah. I just realized I forgot to ask my mom if it was okay that you came over."

"Oh! Do you think I should go?"

"No, it's fine. I'll just tell her when she's off the phone."

"Okay."

"Are you hungry?"

Charlie nodded.

"I'll make us some sandwiches. Here, you can sit down." I led him, a little awkwardly, to the kitchen island, and he sat down on a stool while I rummaged around in the fridge. "Do you like peanut butter and jelly?"

"Yeah."

"Good, because that's pretty much all I know how to make," I said.

Mom walked into the kitchen then. "Sorry about that, honey. Hi. Are you Charlie?"

Charlie nodded and smiled in the direction of my mom and shifted uncomfortably on his stool.

"It's nice to meet you!" she said.

"It's nice to meet you, too, Mrs. Grant," he said. "Sorry I just kind of showed up—"

"Not at all. It's good to meet one of Olivia's new friends."

"I forgot to ask if it was okay if he came over," I said hurriedly. "You were gone or else I would have and—"

"It's fine, Olivia." She smiled, and I knew it was, but all of a sudden I wondered if forgetting to ask her about Charlie was something that belonged on my Neverdo List. What if a lot of things I hadn't worried about before were the beginnings of autistic behaviors? I needed to be careful about everything.

"Who were you talking to on the phone?" I asked.

"Your brother's therapist." She gave a small smile. But this time her smile told me we were done talking about it. Especially in front of Charlie.

I didn't ask anything more.

The first time Jacob was evaluated, a lady from the county came to our house. Her primary focus was on Jacob, but every now and then I felt like she was watching me, too. I did everything I could to make sure I was as normal as possible—as different from Jacob as I could possibly be, because I didn't want her to look at me the way she looked at him.

Now I wondered if Mom had said something to her about me—about the possibility of latent autism in siblings.

After that first visit, all the reports confirmed that Jacob was autistic and that he was somewhere near the middle of the spectrum. The psychologist suggested we might try changing some things to make it easier for Jacob, and we did. We changed the kinds of food we ate and didn't eat, because some foods upset his system or made him react more emotionally. We changed the places we went and how we got there, because some environments made

Jacob more prone to meltdowns, and because he had certain issues being in the car. But other things changed, too. The time we spent with therapists and doctors increased a lot those few months after.

The thought of having Jacob evaluated again, finding out more things, and changing more about our lives made me sick to my stomach.

"You want some milk, Olivia?"

"Oh, um, sure," I said. "Thanks."

Mom poured us some milk from the fridge, and I tried my best to bring my thoughts back into the kitchen.

Charlie told stories about the zoo while we ate. But I couldn't shake the feeling that time was starting to press down on us, like a giant hand, squeezing hard.

In my head, I saw myself giving the toy ostrich to my brother once we'd found it and standing there, watching as he kind of woke up. I could see him holding it in both hands, staring at it for a minute. Then he'd recognize it and remember. And some part of his brain—the part that had shifted when he first lost that ostrich—would shift back. He would blink a few times and then look around at Dad and Mom and me.

"What happened?" he'd ask, and we would sit down and tell him. We'd cry a little, and hug each other, but in the end, my brother would be his old self, like before. Everything would be okay. And I would be okay, too. And no one would be lost anymore.

I was anxious to start searching.

Suddenly Jacob came into the kitchen. He'd been building with Legos in his room and had no idea Charlie was here until now.

"Jacob, this is Charlie," Mom said, her voice calm. "Are you ready for some lunch?"

But Jacob was staring at Charlie. Jacob liked knowing things, and he hadn't known there would be a strange boy in the kitchen before he came in for lunch.

Charlie shifted on his stool. Could he feel Jacob's stare?

"Hey, Jacob," Charlie said. "It's nice to meet you."

"It's nice to meet you," Jacob echoed. And he sat down on the stool next to Charlie as if he'd known him his whole life. "Did you know," he asked, turning to Charlie, "that the world's most expensive coffee is made from beans that have been partially digested by the Asian palm civet? They are also called toddy cats. They eat the coffee berries and then poop out the beans. Those beans are roasted and ground into coffee, and sold for as much as 450 dollars a pound."

Charlie almost snorted milk through his nose. Mom started laughing, and then I was laughing, and Jacob was laughing, too, though I don't think he really understood why.

"I didn't know that, Jacob," Charlie said once he'd caught his breath. "That is awesome!"

Jacob smiled and continued. "Did you also know the leaves of deciduous trees aren't really green? The chlorophyll in the leaves acts as a kind of disguise all summer long while the trees are transforming sunlight into food. But in the fall, when all the sugar goes back into the tree's roots, the colors left behind—red, gold, amber, citron, and saffron—are that tree's actual colors."

"Wow! I didn't know that," I said.

"Me neither," said Charlie as he smiled and took a bite of his sandwich.

"Can you imagine being those bright colors all year long but having to keep it a secret so you could stay alive?" I really couldn't.

Charlie shook his head. Jacob poked at his sandwich.

"Okay. My turn," said Charlie. "Did you know that braille isn't a language? It's a tactile alphabet that can be used to write almost any language. There are braille versions of Chinese, Spanish, Arabic, Hebrew, and many other languages, too."

"So cool!" I said.

"I knew that," said Jacob.

Mom gave a small smile.

The rest of lunch went great. Jacob didn't melt down over a single thing. He actually seemed more normal than he'd been in a while. Charlie seemed to have a way of knowing what people needed. Maybe he was good at reading people's emotions because he couldn't get distracted by their clothes or faces and stuff. He just *heard* what we were saying and how we were saying it, and voices are bad at disguising things.

Jacob was perceptive, too. He knew there was something

different about Charlie right away, and when Charlie told him he was blind, neither of them were weird about it. They were just themselves. It was easy to be together, there in the kitchen. It wasn't awkward or scary or weird at all. But maybe that's what happens when people agree to let each other be just exactly who they are—no pretending.

After we finished lunch, Mom asked Charlie and me what we had planned for the afternoon.

"We're working on a project," I said hurriedly.

"What kind of project?"

"Well, it's kind of a surprise. I don't really want to talk about it yet," I said.

Charlie looked confused about why we weren't saying anything, but he just nodded in agreement. Jacob sat there quietly, breaking the crust on his plate into smaller and smaller pieces.

"A surprise project? Well, that sounds mysterious!" Mom looked amused. But I didn't feel like smiling back. I didn't want her to think it was silly, or a waste of time. I didn't want her to say anything about it at all. It was too important.

I gave a small shrug.

"All right. Have fun, but don't forget, we'll need to leave for play practice by four thirty, okay?"

I'd kept the butterflies calm all day, but now they swirled around in my stomach again. Some of my excitement shifted to worry.

"Do you really think I can do this?"

Mom thought about it for a minute. "I do," she said. "Part of being in a play is trusting the director to choose the right people for the right parts and to direct the best play ever. Right?"

"Yeah, I guess."

"So, why don't you trust Stephen and Dorothy to do their job, and you just focus on being the best Peter Pan you can be."

I nodded and smiled. "Okay."

"You'll be great," Charlie chimed in, and Mom nodded.

"You'll be great!" Jacob echoed.

My smile faltered. I wanted to believe that. I wished I could wrap their encouraging words around myself like a blanket and stay there all warm and safe. But then I remembered latent autism. It crawled out of the corner of my mind and hung over me like an invisible sign. What if I was the farthest thing from *great*? What if I ended up having a meltdown of my own? Or ended up doing things that belonged on my Neverdo List?

I tried to push the thoughts away. For now, all I could do was my best, like Mom said.

I led Charlie to my room so we could put the finishing touches on our map and figure out where we should begin our new search. But I couldn't stop thinking about what I needed to add to my list. It was hard, trying to decide if something even belonged on it or not. In my head, I listed everything I could think of so I wouldn't forget to write them down as soon as Charlie left.

Neverdo List, Entry #2

1. Never forget to tell Mom when I'm bringing friends over.

2. Never slam my bedroom door.

3. Never get too nervous.

18

....

The Best Kid for the Job

AFTER WE FINISHED the map, and Charlie left, we got into the car and drove to Tulsa.

Now it was five o'clock, and the first rehearsal was about to start. Jacob was fidgeting two seats over. He had needed an empty seat on either side of him. He seemed almost as nervous as I was. But hopefully having Mom here would help.

"All right, everyone. Please join us onstage and make a big circle," said Dorothy.

Jacob and I made our way up. There were about twenty-five of us, and every kid here had been given a part. One by one, we introduced ourselves and the parts we would be playing. Some were pirates, some were Indians, others were mermaids or animals. And of course, there were the Lost Boys, like Jacob.

Finally, it was my turn. "Hi. My name is Olivia Grant, and I'm playing the part of Peter Pan."

Everyone was quiet for a minute. And then one of the Lost Boys spoke up.

"A girl? A *girl* can't play Peter Pan!"

A few others laughed.

I looked around the circle. Some kids looked confused. Some were nodding their heads. I found Mom's eyes in the audience. She mouthed, "It's okay." But it wasn't.

Stephen looked around the circle, too. "Does anyone else here think a girl shouldn't be playing the part of Peter Pan?" he asked.

A few kids raised their hands.

"I see," he said.

Stephen looked at Dorothy. She nodded back. They were going to change their minds right there and let someone else play the part of Peter. I knew it.

I felt my palms start to sweat. This was a mistake. I shouldn't have come. I rubbed my arms and felt goose bumps prickle my skin. I wanted to run offstage, or hide, or something. But that was something Jacob would have done. That was a neverdo. So, I held still, standing as tall and steady as I could.

Stephen tucked his clipboard under his arm. "Okay. Well, this is a good thing to talk about, and I need all of us to be on the same page about this one. So, have a seat."

We all sat down in our circle formation and I swallowed hard, trying to hold back the tears and the lump that was rising in my throat. I never should have agreed to play Peter.

"Who can tell me something about Peter Pan, besides the fact that you think his character is supposed to be played by a boy?"

Hands started going up, and Stephen pointed at each person.

"He's brave."

"He's strong!"

"He can fight with a sword!"

"He saves his friends."

"He's funny."

"He can fly!"

"He never grows up!"

Stephen nodded at each of these answers.

"He can crow like a rooster."

Stephen turned to me.

"Olivia, can you crow for me?"

"Err-err-err-err errrrrrr!" I gave my very best rooster impression and crowed loudly. It was actually even better than my audition.

"So, what you're all telling me," said Stephen, "is that Peter Pan has to be played by someone who can act brave, strong, funny, and kind, and can fight with a sword, fly, look out for others, and crow like a rooster."

Everyone nodded.

"Okay," Stephen said. He walked around the inside of the circle, thinking, his hands behind his back. "Can any of you tell me about the parts you've been given? You—who are you in the play?" Stephen pointed to a boy who was sitting across the circle from me.

"I'm the Neverbird," the boy said. And he stood up and flapped his arms very convincingly. Everyone laughed. My brother laughed the longest and the hardest. He laughed until Stephen gently said his name and asked him to quiet down. Kids were staring and whispering. Jacob was making things worse already. The stage felt like it was crushing in on me. I wanted the curtain to fall.

I looked at Mom; she was watching us.

See? I said with my eyes. *It's only the first practice and already Jacob is ruining things!*

Shhh, she said with her eyes. *It's going to be okay.* So I just sat quietly, waiting for whatever came next.

Stephen stood in the center of the circle, his face serious. "So, Walter here is the Neverbird," he said. "But, well, don't you guys think that part should be played by, you know, a *bird*? I mean, an actual bird is the best at being a bird, right?"

No one said a word.

Dorothy smiled. Stephen smiled.

"I'm kidding, of course," he continued. "Why can't this part be played by a bird?"

We all looked around at one another.

"Can anyone tell me?" Stephen asked.

Finally, one girl raised her hand. "Because a real bird can't do all the things that you need the Neverbird to do in this play."

"Bingo! Would you all agree that Dorothy and I chose Walter over there to be the Neverbird because we believe he is going to be the best Neverbird this play has ever seen, even though he's not an *actual bird*?"

Everyone laughed and said yes in chorus.

"Good," Stephen said. "And can you also agree that Dorothy and I chose Olivia to play the part of Peter Pan because we felt she was capable of being the best version of a brave, strong, funny, kind boy who can sword fight, fly, look out for others, and crow like a rooster?"

The room got quiet again. But most of the cast nodded.

"Excellent. And you know, the part of Peter Pan is traditionally played by a woman." Stephen winked at me. Dorothy nodded. Relief washed over my whole self. They still thought I could do this. In spite of what the other kids thought. And in spite of Jacob.

"So! Who's ready to read some lines?" Dorothy said. She held up a huge stack of papers all stapled together, and everyone raised eager hands. "These are your scripts. And they are very important, so please don't lose them. You will be expected to have your lines memorized in four weeks. So, you'll need to start working on them as soon as you can."

Everyone nodded.

"One by one, as I call your names, I want you to come up, take your script, and introduce yourself to the group again, this time as the character you'll be playing—in the *voice* of that character. And I want you to strike a position you think that character would make. Okay? Everyone understand? Let's start with you, Olivia."

I closed my eyes and buried thoughts of latent autism and missing ostriches and neverdos. I imagined Peter Pan, who never wants to grow up. That brave, strong, funny, kind boy who can sword fight, fly, look out for others, and crow like a rooster. He came alive inside my mind. I knew how he would stand and walk. How he might smile, his eyes flashing and all his teeth showing. I put him on like a costume—like my favorite sweatshirt. And then I opened my eyes, jumped to my feet, and leapt to center stage.

Dorothy handed me my script. I spun on my heel and called out as loud as I could, "I'm Peter Pan!"

Then I put my hands on my hips and crowed like a rooster, and this time, everyone clapped.

19

....

Watch and Notice

FOR THE REST of the week, whenever I wasn't doing my hours at the zoo or rehearsing for Peter Pan, I was searching for lost things.

Mrs. Mackenelli's glasses went missing, and I found them in her bread drawer.

Our neighbor Mr. Anderson lost his car keys on Tuesday and then his wallet on Wednesday. I found them both.

Mom lost an earring Wednesday night, and I found it in the driveway. I even found the tiny gold back.

"You're getting rather famous for your finding skills!" Dad said. "You should start charging for your services."

If I could find Jacob's missing ostrich, maybe it would be worth thinking about.

For now, Charlie and I were still focused on searching.

After my Responsibility Hours were finished at the zoo on Thursday, we walked the nine blocks into town and went to the library.

First we asked the librarian about a missing toy ostrich.

"A missing what?" He furrowed his eyebrows at us over the rim of his glasses.

"A toy ostrich," I said again. I held up two fingers, showing him about how big it was. "My brother lost it about seven months ago, and I'm trying to find it."

"And you think he lost it here?"

"Maybe?" I shrugged. "I looked here once before, months ago, but I don't think I looked hard enough."

"Well, I'm sorry, but I don't think I've seen anything like the item you're describing," said the librarian. "You're welcome to check the lost and found table, though." But we already had, and it wasn't there.

"Do you mind if we search around in the stacks?" Charlie asked. The librarian stared at Charlie, who obviously couldn't see. Charlie waited patiently, sunglasses on and cane in hand.

"We'll be very quiet and make sure nothing gets out of order," I promised.

The librarian sighed. "All right, fine. But please be careful."

So, we started searching the stacks. Prue's library is very small, but even tiny libraries have a lot of bookshelves. The children's section took about two hours to search with both Charlie and me reaching between each book and behind the rows to check the empty space between the pages and the bookshelf wall.

All we found was a bookmark, three paper clips, and someone's notes on Mount Kilimanjaro.

We found even less in the adult section. Just a dried-out ball-point pen and a slip of paper with reference numbers scrawled across the top. But no ostriches.

After a few hours of searching, I walked Charlie back to the zoo, still upset. Then I trudged home slowly, through the yard, up the front porch steps, and inside, letting the door slam behind me.

"I hate the stupid library. I can never find what I'm looking for!" I was frustrated. But then, as I came into the kitchen, I saw a strange woman there, leaning over my brother at the kitchen table while Mom watched. They were working on a puzzle or something.

I froze. All my frustration over my brother's missing ostrich settled in the pit of my stomach.

"Oh, no! I'm sorry! I—I'm so sorry—sorry!—I'm—"

The lady looked up and smiled at me.

Jacob looked up and smiled at me.

Mom looked up, but she didn't smile. Her eyes were full of questions. I was overreacting. A neverdo. Things started to feel all twisty inside me. I could tell it was showing on my face.

"Olivia, this is Dr. Kathy Martin," Mom said.

I swallowed hard and tried to smile. I just needed to calm down. But all I could think about was what had happened the last time Mom had had Jacob evaluated. And I kept seeing that article on her desk.

"Nice to meet you," I said. I cleared my throat. "I'm Olivia. Sorry I burst in like that. I didn't mean to interrupt."

That was good. That sounded normal.

Dr. Kathy rose in her chair and stuck out her hand. A handshake. I suddenly felt panicky. I looked away from her, at Mom, out the window, then quickly shook her hand before stuffing both of mine into my pockets.

"I was outside and at the library, and stuff. My hands are dirty—I, uh, need to wash—" I wanted to get out of there. I didn't want her to pay any more attention to me. I was worried she'd somehow be able to tell how close I was to being just like Jacob. Because that was her job, after all. To observe and diagnose.

"Oh, that's fine," Dr. Kathy smiled.

"Oh, that's fine!" echoed Jacob from behind her. "Come see what I'm working on, Olivia." Jacob pointed at the puzzle on the table. Piles of tiny puzzle pieces were arranged by color around him, and Jacob was meticulously fitting them together, one after the other, like he'd done this puzzle a hundred times before.

"Wow! Nice work," I said. And it really was. He was amazing at puzzles.

"Did you know puzzles were designed by mapmakers?" Jacob asked. "They made careful copies of their maps and pasted them on wood and then cut them into pieces. It helped them to memorize areas they had already mapped, and it was a way to teach mapmaking apprentices how different areas of land fit together."

I blinked. "Wow, I didn't know that," I said. "Thanks, Jacob."

He smiled. "You're welcome, Olivia."

"Do you like puzzles, too, Olivia?" asked Dr. Kathy.

I shook my head. I knew it was her job to interact with the whole family, because we all interacted with Jacob, but I didn't want to.

"It's okay, Olivia," Mom said.

"Um, no, not really. I'm not very good at them. I'm better at finding missing things."

"Well, even that is a kind of puzzle," she said. "You have to gather clues and put pieces of information together."

I cleared my throat. It felt like she was looking inside my head. Like somehow she knew about the map, and Jacob's missing ostrich, and my desperate need to find it.

I had to get out of there.

"Excuse me." Manners are important when you are trying to be normal. "I'm going to go, um, wash my hands." I held them up like they were crawling with germs. "Nice to meet you, Dr. Kathy."

"It was nice to meet you, too, Olivia. I'm sure I'll see you again." She smiled, but I couldn't smile back. I didn't want to see her again. I wanted her to go away. I wanted Jacob to be fine. Better. Normal. And *I* wanted to be normal. I had to fix this.

I had to find that ostrich.

I felt Mom's eyes on my back as I walked calmly out of the kitchen and down the hall to the bathroom. I washed my hands in record time and grabbed my backpack from my room.

"I'm going to the zoo, Mom!" I called into the kitchen. "I need to tell Charlie something!"

"Okay," Mom called back. I left through the back door without letting it slam behind me. Very normal. But once I was sure I was out of eyesight, I bolted through the backyard and down the minimal maintenance road.

I ran all the way to the zoo, through the open gate, across the parking lot, behind the ticket office building, and over to the trailer where Charlie and his mom lived. I pounded on the door until he opened it.

"We-need-to-find-Jacob's-ostrich!" I was out of breath, and the words came out in a long, superfast stream. "Now!"

"Well, hello to you, too, Olivia. Didn't I just see you a little bit ago?" He stood in the doorway, tilting his head and kind of laughing at me.

"Sorry," I said. "Hi again." A normal greeting. Sort of. I was glad he couldn't see me, because I was sweating, and the humidity had made my curly hair more wild than usual. There were leaves in it, too, because I'd taken a shortcut through the underbrush to get there faster. I looked crazy.

"Can we do a little more searching? Please? It's kind of an emergency."

Charlie nodded. "Yeah. Sure. Hang on a second, I have to get my cane and let Mom know I'm leaving." He stepped back inside and then whirled around. "Um, where, exactly, are we going?"

"I don't know yet," I said. "Probably back to my house? I want to look around in the yard and stuff."

Charlie nodded and went back inside. When he came out just a few minutes later, he was wearing his backpack and holding his cane. Vera stepped out onto the porch and evaluated us.

"Charlie has my phone," she said. "If you need anything, feel free to call the house, okay?"

I nodded and tried not to stare at her tattoos. She was in a grey T-shirt and jeans, which looked strange because I was so used to seeing her in her zoo uniform.

"Mom. It's fine. I'll be fine. We'll just be at Olivia's house. Her mom is home. I'll call if we need anything." He reached out and took hold of my arm. "Is it okay if I hold on to you? Sometimes it's faster if you can, like, lead. I can hear where you're walking, feel my way a little easier. Is that okay?"

"Yeah! Yes. Totally fine. Here."

I let him hold on to my arm, and we started walking back toward my house. It was a little strange. Not like holding hands or anything, because he needed my help. But it felt good. Like we were showing each other the way.

"So, what's going on?" Charlie asked as he hurried beside me. "I know finding Jacob's ostrich is important and everything, but we already spent like three hours searching the library today."

We were barely through the gate back down the road toward my house, but we were already both a little out of breath because

I was in such a rush. I knew Charlie was right. I probably seemed crazy. But the minute I'd seen Dr. Kathy Martin leaning over my brother, I'd known we had to keep going.

"We have to keep looking!"

"Did something happen? You seem really upset."

I felt a lump growing in the back of my throat, and I swallowed hard.

"Mom decided Jacob needed to be reevaluated. And when I got home, a psychologist was sitting at the kitchen table with him."

"Is that bad?"

"It could be."

"Why?"

"Because the last time he was evaluated, everything changed. The way we did everything—what we ate, how we spent our time—we had to make sure everything worked for Jacob. Now that he's getting worse, other things will have to happen. Even bigger changes. Treatments and therapies. And if all that can happen to Jacob, then it could happen to me, too! I mean . . ." I trailed off. But it was too late. I'd said it out loud.

"Wait, what? What are you talking about? What do you think could happen to you?"

"Nothing. I—never mind. Come on. Let's just go."

"Olivia, it's not nothing!" Charlie planted himself in the middle of the road, and he wasn't moving. "Why do you think you'll need the same kind of treatment as Jacob? I thought you said you couldn't catch autism. Didn't you say it was something you're born with?"

"I did. And that's true."

"So, then what is it?"

I tried, but I couldn't get any more words out. I wasn't ready for Charlie to know about the article, and latent autism. It would change everything. And I couldn't handle any more change right now.

"It's nothing. I'm fine." I swallowed hard.

Charlie looked at me like he knew I was most definitely not fine, but he didn't say anything else about it. He just slipped his hand back around my arm. Only this time, it felt more like he was leading me.

We were both quiet the rest of the way. When we finally reached my backyard, Charlie spoke.

"So, where do you want to start?"

"Well, I've already searched everywhere inside the house, and I didn't find anything useful. And I've searched the garage and the shed, too," I said. "How about right here in the yard? Then we can officially check my house off the map."

"You don't think you would have found it already if it was right here in the yard?"

I looked around. "Well, there's a lot of long grass around the edge of the property. Maybe he dropped it there and I just missed it?" I shrugged. "I don't know. I just want to cross my house off the list and it's the last place around here I can think to look."

"Okay." Charlie nodded and started making his way around the near side of the yard, sweeping his cane in front of him as he went, tapping it against trees. Feeling out the space. I took the far side and started searching the long grass that separated our yard from state land.

So much depended on this. So much depended on me being able to find that little toy ostrich, and there were so many places it could be.

Found things only have one place, and they fill that space up to the top. But lost things can be anywhere. It was overwhelming.

After just fifteen minutes, I told Charlie I needed a break. I sat down.

"What's the matter?" he asked.

I sighed. "Nothing."

He followed my voice and walked over.

"That's the fourth time you've done that."

"Done what?"

He let out a huge sigh.

"Oh."

"So, what's the matter?" Charlie sat down beside me.

"This just feels really hard."

"Well, it is."

"I know. But I mean, it feels *too* hard."

Charlie nodded. "Can I ask you a question?"

"Sure," I said.

"What are you hoping will change once you find Jacob's toy? I know you said you think it will help . . . but help with what, exactly?"

This was the hard part. Putting words around what this meant and felt like to me. But I had to try.

"Things were just so much better before Jacob lost his ostrich. It was such a comfort to him. I know if I can find it, things will be a little easier for all of us. Give us another chance at being a more normal family."

"A more normal family?"

"Yeah. A family where people don't act crazy and scary, and where they don't throw things all the time. The kind of family that can go places without someone having a meltdown, or screaming and crying, or whatever. Where we don't have to do things in any particular way and we can just get in the car and drive on the main roads at a normal speed and not have to think about whether we're going to a place that will be too crowded or not. The kind of family that doesn't need doctors and therapists to come to the house so they can watch and observe and see how we're all doing . . . stuff like that."

Charlie didn't say anything for so long I started to wonder if he'd heard me.

"So, just to be sure I'm getting this straight, you want the kind of family where everyone is healthy? And where you can do stuff together, and go places together, and everyone behaves themselves, and no one gets too worked up?"

"Yeah, I guess . . ." It wasn't exactly what I'd said, but it wasn't untrue, either.

Charlie kept going.

"So, *not* like the kind of family that lives at a zoo, and where someone is, you know, *blind* or anything? Normal like that?"

Charlie's voice had gone sharp now. And hurt. I suddenly realized what he *thought* I'd been saying—not just about my family but about his. And about him.

"What? No!" I said. "No! I didn't mean—"

"I think I know what you meant, Olivia." Charlie stood up from where he'd been sitting beside me in the grass. "I get it. It's okay. I know what it's like to want things to be normal, too. And to try to do everything you can to make it that way. Believe me. I really, really get it. But life doesn't work that way."

He paused, and we were both quiet.

"You know," Charlie said finally, "I think I'm going to let you finish this on your own today. I don't think I'd be very much help anyway."

"Yes, you will! I need your help! Please, Charlie. I'm really sorry. I didn't mean that about you. I want—"

"You want *normal*. Right? Well, I'm sorry, but that's not me. I'll see you later."

Charlie shook the linked pieces of his cane into place and put one foot in front of the other.

I wanted to ask him to stop, to please stay, but I couldn't say anything, because a huge lump was stuck in my throat. So, I just watched him walk out of the yard and back down the minimal maintenance road, sweeping his cane in front of him as he went.

20

Stranded

CHARLIE DIDN'T COME around the next morning at the zoo. I'd hoped everything would be fine, that he just needed time to believe I was telling the truth when I'd said I hadn't meant to hurt his feelings. But I couldn't find him anywhere. That made my Responsibility Hours, and my tasks that day—raking out the donkeys' enclosure, replenishing the straw in the Komodo dragon's area—go by even slower than usual. And it made concentrating at rehearsal that afternoon harder, too.

At play practice we were just starting to block some of the larger group scenes. We were all still reading off our scripts, of course, but Dorothy assigned each of us a place to stand while we read our lines. It made things feel real.

We were working on a scene where the Lost Boys argue about who's the best at being a Lost Boy.

"I'm pretty sure Peter thinks I'm the best," said Curly.

"No way!" Nibs elbowed his way in front of Curly. "I'm better at fighting bears than you are!"

"Well, neither of you can sing, and Peter loves when I sing," said Slightly, who broke into song.

"Hold on!" shouted Tootles. "I am the fastest! Peter can't fight pirates without me! See?" And Tootles pulled a sword from his belt and ran circles around the rest of the boys to prove how fast he was.

Jacob was one of the twins, and he just copied exactly what his stage brother said all the time.

"Well, Peter likes me best because there's two of me!" shouted Twin One over the noise of the other boys.

Then there was a long pause.

Jacob was supposed to echo Twin One. But instead he was standing a little apart from the group, waving at me where I stood in the wings. I didn't want to break character, so I rushed onstage like Peter was supposed to.

"Boys! Boys! You're all my favorite!" I insisted, running into the fray to break up the fighting and keep them from starting a wrestling match.

"You're all my favorite!" echoed Jacob, copying me instead of his stage twin. Of course everyone laughed. But not because the line was funny, or the acting was funny, but because my brother was strange and unpredictable.

We ran the end of the scene twice until Jacob understood which line he was supposed to echo. He didn't seem bothered by it at all. But it was awkward and uncomfortable for me, and I kept wondering why on earth anyone had agreed to let Jacob play the part in the first place.

I sighed and turned my attention back to Dorothy.

"Olivia," she said, glancing at her clipboard and the stack of director's notes. "Let's run the scene where you and Amelia are stranded, just after the fight with Hook when he and his first mate row off laughing. Here—" She gestured to me and patted the top of the large wooden box on stage right. "Why don't you sit here, and Amelia, you sit beside her." Dorothy positioned us. "Now, when we do this for real, this box will be a rock and you'll be surrounded by water with the tide rising. Peter and Wendy are about to be stranded. Imagine waves rising all around you and no help in sight. Amelia, why don't you start with your line on page thirty-seven: 'Peter! You're hurt!'"

"Peter! You're hurt!" Amelia read her line and I bent over, pretending I actually was. But all it did was remind me again about how I'd hurt Charlie for real.

"I'll be all right, Wendy," I read my line, trying to put all the emotion into it that I could. "But I'm afraid I can't fly off this rock. I can't save you, Wendy."

"Oh, Peter! Whatever shall we do?" Amelia buried her face in her hands and started to cry.

"Good!" Dorothy clapped for us. "Now, this is the part where the kite trails in—" Dorothy gestured toward the hook and tackle in the ceiling overhead. "Olivia, you'll secure the string of the kite to Amelia's harness, and the kite will fly her to safety offstage."

Then we ran that scene, too, pretending I save Wendy with the last hope of rescue either of us have. And because the kite isn't strong enough to carry us both, Wendy sails offstage while I'm left on the rock, wounded, about to be swept away by the waves and eaten by the Tick-Tock Croc. Except, of course, I'm unexpectedly rescued, too.

But while I sat there, waiting for the Neverbird to float by on his massive raft of a nest and sail me to safety, the loneliness under the lights felt so real I had to fight to hold back tears. I knew what it was like to watch your last hope for rescue, and your last friend, sail away without you.

Neverdo List, Entry #3

1. Never freak out when Dr. Kathy, or any company, is here.

2. Never act all crazy.

3. Never hurt anyone's feelings, even by accident.

21

Broken Glass

"SO, HOW WAS rehearsal today?" Dad asked when we got home.

I didn't want to talk about rehearsal because it didn't matter how it had gone. Jacob had still been evaluated, and his ostrich was still missing, and Charlie was still mad at me.

In my head, I kept hearing my brother repeating the wrong lines onstage.

"Fine," I mumbled.

Dad cleared his throat.

"Okay then . . . well, how did the evaluation go?" He stabbed his fork through another piece of spinach, and I pushed mine around on my plate. I had completely lost my appetite, and I didn't want to talk about any of this. Every time I closed my eyes, I saw Charlie walking away, sweeping the grass with his cane.

"I'm not sure," Mom said. "Good, I think? Jacob seemed to have fun. Did you have fun, Jacob?" My brother sat beside me at the table, his hands clenched tightly in his lap. At the moment, he didn't look like he was having very much fun at all.

"I don't like dinner," he said. "I prefer breakfast."

Dad laughed. But Jacob wasn't trying to be funny. Mom shook her head at Dad a tiny bit. Jacob didn't like to be laughed at. But it was too late. He looked at Dad and then at Mom. His face was very serious. Very urgent. Like he needed them to understand something important.

"I prefer breakfast!" He took a deep breath. "I prefer breakfast! *I prefer breakfast!*" His voice was loud and high-pitched, and the knot in my stomach clenched. He yelled it again. Mom and Dad looked at each other. They knew what to do. They would handle things. Except they weren't quite fast enough this time. I watched as Jacob's arm arced back and then flew forward, releasing his glass of milk like a perfect pitch across home plate. The glass shattered against the wall, sending a spray of milk and shards of glass everywhere. They hit the dining room floor in a tinkling shower.

No one said anything for the space of a breath. And then Jacob screamed.

"Ahhhhhhhhhhhhhh!"

Mom jumped out of her chair. Dad hollered and waved his arms, frustrated and upset, and Jacob melted down, pounding his fists on things and screaming "I prefer breakfast!" over and over. He lurched out of his chair and banged his head against the wall— once, twice, three times. Dad tried to pull him out of the dining room and away from all the glass.

I eased out of my chair. I just wanted to get out of there. I wanted to be somewhere quiet where nothing was broken or ruined or lost. I walked quickly away from the table.

"Owwwwwwww!"

I stopped. Suddenly there was blood—my blood—and a lot of it. My foot hurt like a million fires and my chest hurt from trying to hold myself together all day.

"What? What?!" Mom said frantically.

"I'm bleeding!"

Mom whirled around, and Dad let go of Jacob, who fell to the floor, wailing. My brother didn't stop screaming or calm down at all, even when he saw that I was bleeding and crying. He only got louder.

"I'm bleeding!" Jacob wailed, copying me. "I'm bleeding!"

When Mom knelt down beside me, her capable I-can-take-care-of-this face crumpled. She shook her head for a minute, and then she started crying, too. Right there beside me in the middle of all that blood and broken glass and spilled milk.

"I'm sorry," she whispered. "I'm so sorry, honey. Here, let me see?" But I didn't want her to see, or touch it because it hurt too much. I could feel the piece of glass bite and grate underneath my skin whenever I moved. Getting it out was going to hurt. More than it did already. I cried harder just thinking about it.

And then Dad got down to business. He scooped me up and set me on the couch. Then he pulled Jacob to his feet and hauled him off to his room to calm him down. Mom pulled the medical kit out from its spot under the kitchen sink. She held my hand and rubbed my back and helped me soak my foot in hot water.

Eventually, Dad came back in. "He's okay now," Dad said. "He's resting."

Mom breathed a sigh of relief, and Dad used the tweezers to take out the piece of glass. It hurt so bad that I cried until I couldn't catch my breath. I was not even a tiny bit brave. But three Band-Aids, a strip of gauze, iodine for disinfectant, and a dish of strawberry ice cream helped, a little.

"It's all Jacob's fault."

I didn't even realize I had said the words out loud until I saw the look in Mom's eyes. It was only there for a second. Like I'd hurt her. Cut *her* with glass. But it was true. None of this would have happened if it hadn't been for my brother. I didn't regret saying it, but I felt bad that it had hurt my mom. Truth does that sometimes. There's the nice truth and the not-so-nice truth. This time it felt good to tell the not-so-nice kind.

After I'd finished my ice cream and Mom and Dad had cleaned up the mess of glass and milk and blood, Dad said it was bedtime. I probably could have hobbled to my room on my own, but Dad picked me up, and I let him carry me. Mom went to check on Jacob.

"I used to carry you around like this when you were itty-bitty," he said, rubbing his whiskery face against my cheek.

"Dad!" His face was scratchy, and I felt too old for his teasing.

But I let him do it anyway. He even did a little spin in front of my bedroom door before he plopped me down on my bed.

"You need anything? Water? Tylenol? A pony?"

I gave a small smile. "Definitely a pony."

But all I really needed, all I really wanted, more than my foot to feel better, more than being Peter Pan, more than making sure Charlie and I were still friends, was for things to go back to the way they were before, when everything was easier and Jacob was better. But Dad couldn't help me with that any more than he could make a pony appear in the middle of my bedroom.

"Hey, Dad . . . ?" I wanted to tell him that I knew about latent autism. But I couldn't do that without letting on that I was still looking for Jacob's ostrich and that I wouldn't let it stay missing. That I was going to make everything so much better. So, I couldn't say anything. Not yet.

"Um . . . could you maybe get me some Tylenol?"

"Sure." He walked out of the room, and I put on my pajamas, being careful of my foot. Then I opened my bedroom window and climbed back into bed.

Dad returned with a glass of water and two Tylenol. He pulled the covers up around my chin and kissed my forehead.

"You know your window is open?" he said.

"Yeah. I like it open."

"But the screen is out, honey. I'm a little nervous some critter is going to crawl into your bedroom while you're sleeping."

"It's okay," I insisted. "I'll be fine." But the whole time I was thinking about Ethel and wondering what my parents would think if they knew an ostrich had been wandering into our backyard.

"Wait!" I sat up in bed. "I have to call Vera and let her know I won't be able to work at the zoo tomorrow."

"Your mom or I will call her," Dad said. "Don't worry. She'll understand."

"Can you ask her to tell Charlie, too?"

"Charlie. Check. Anything else?"

I thought about it for a minute. "Nope. That's it. Thanks. Love you."

"Love you, too, Olivia. Good night."

"Night."

The curtains fluttered lightly in the open window as he closed the door.

Neverdo List, Entry #4

1. Never freak out about stuff when I could be brave instead.

2. Never say hurtful things to Mom.

22

....

A Hard Walk

SOMETIME DURING THE night, I sat straight up in bed, my heart pounding, trying to catch my breath. I'd dreamed Jacob had thrown Ethel against the dining room wall. She'd smashed into a million pieces and covered the room in so many feathers, we'd started breathing them in, choking and coughing. I kept trying to pull feathers out of my mouth, but they wouldn't stop coming.

I blinked in the darkness and ran my tongue over my teeth. No feathers. Not a single one. No broken birds anywhere in sight.

The wind blew the curtains around. Something was out in the yard. I jumped out of bed.

"Ow! *Owowowow!*" I had completely forgotten about my foot. I hopped over to the window and there was Ethel, just standing there.

This was the third time she'd shown up since I'd started working at the zoo. I leaned out the window. The giant bird cocked her head at me, like she was waiting.

"Now what?" I whispered. I had to be quiet. The last thing I wanted was for Mom or Dad to come in and see the ostrich in the backyard. "What do you want? Why are you here?"

Ethel didn't answer me. She just reached her long neck to the ground and pecked at something I couldn't see.

Could I walk her back to the zoo? I tested some weight on my foot. It still hurt. But if I walked on my toes and hopped a little bit, I could probably do it. So, I cracked open my bedroom door, peeked out, and listened. I could hear Dad was snoring, but besides that everything else was quiet.

My hoodie was in the closet, and I didn't want the squeaky door to wake anyone up, so I limped into the kitchen and pulled down Jacob's hoodie from its hook on the wall. Carefully, I limped back down the hall to Mom and Dad's closed bedroom door and whispered what I had the last time I brought Ethel back to the zoo in the middle of the night.

And then I went back to my room and crawled out the window. Slowly. Painfully.

The grass was wet with dew and soaked through my shoes quickly. Ethel waited as I limped toward her.

"What am I going to do with you?" I asked. She blinked at me. The yard light cast our deep shadows across the grass. Tall and distorted. If Ethel had been a dog or a pony, I might have patted her neck or something. And even though she'd been part of a petting zoo back in Tulsa, I felt weird about petting her. Her legs were strong enough to kill an attacking lion with a single kick—that was her superpower, that and her running speed—and I didn't really want to risk either one of those things. So, I kept my distance.

I stuffed my hands in the pockets of Jacob's hoodie. One of them was already full of Cap'n Crunch. Had I worn Jacob's hoodie the last time Ethel had showed up? I must have forgotten.

"Let's go, you crazy bird," I said, dropping a handful of food on the ground. She probably thought this was the best thing ever. No wonder she kept coming back. Free snacks and a friend to walk home with.

Ethel ate and I hobbled on ahead of her, dropping pieces and leaving a trail for her to follow, all the way down the minimal maintenance road and back to the zoo. It was a very slow walk. Even with taking rests and hopping on one foot now and then, it was hard. And long.

But I kept going until we reached the zoo's front entrance. The gate was wide open, and the light that hung over the door of the office building cast weird shadows. Suddenly I was worried. What if whoever had let her out was here now, watching? With the last bit of food in my pocket, I coaxed Ethel back in and closed the gate behind her.

I waited a minute or two; I couldn't resist looking in the direction of Charlie and Vera's trailer. I hoped they were both still asleep inside. More than that, I wished I could go back and change what I'd said the day before. I wished I could make Charlie understand that I never meant to hurt his feelings.

For now, though, I needed to get home. I was really tired, and I still had a long walk. The cut on my foot pulled and burned under the gauze and Band-Aids. But I walked anyway. Slowly. Mostly on my toes. If only I could fly for real.

When I finally got back to the house, I crawled back through my window, peeled off my wet shoes and socks, and changed into some dry pajamas. Then I closed my eyes, snuggled deep into my pillow, and slept.

Until something woke me up.

"Olivia. Olivia?"

I opened my eyes and my breath caught. He looked different than he had the night before. He wasn't angry or loud or upset. He was just himself. My brother, Jacob. Always full of interesting information and particular about the way he did stuff. But I knew that scary part of him was still in there. The part that had thrown a glass and banged his head against the wall.

"Olivia! Olivia!"

"What? I'm right here, you don't have to yell."

"Happy birthday!" he said.

"It's not my birthday, Jacob." It was nowhere near my birthday.

"Happy birthday for pretend!" he said, and he handed me a small package wrapped perfectly. Every corner creased, every seam perfect. Jacob was good at wrapping gifts.

"He made you something," Mom said, peeking around my

bedroom door. "He wanted to show you that he's sorry about what happened last night."

"Really? Thanks, Jacob."

I took the package from my brother. But I was still a tiny bit nervous. Jacob had never given me a gift before. At least, not one all on his own. He'd given me Christmas presents Mom had bought for him to give to me. But this was different. Then again, he'd never hurt me before, either.

I pulled back the paper, hurrying and tearing off one of the corners. But Jacob's face twisted with frustration, and he grabbed the package out of my hand.

"Be careful, Olivia! Be careful." And then he slowly handed it back. I took it, cautiously. And I gently removed the rest of the paper, watching Jacob as I went. I didn't want to do anything that might upset him or cause another meltdown.

The wrapping revealed a shoe box, and inside was a drawing of an ostrich in green crayon. I looked at Mom and held up the picture so she could see. She nodded. I stared at the drawing, trying to understand what Jacob was saying. Did he know about Ethel? Did he think I liked ostriches? Did he remember that morning in front of the zoo gate? Did he know I was looking for his lost toy?

I smoothed the drawing across my lap. Maybe he was telling me to keep looking. Maybe he was asking for help? Maybe he wanted me to find his missing ostrich.

I wanted to tell Charlie.

I didn't know what to say. "Wow. Thanks, Jacob."

He was excited and kind of jumping around my room, not ruining anything or making a mess, just jumping. Like a little kid at a party.

"Okay, Jacob," Mom said finally. "Let's go make breakfast. You want to help me?" Jacob ran out of the room, and Mom bent over and kissed my forehead. "How's your foot? You slept later than usual."

"It's kinda sore," I said. Actually, it hurt like crazy. I shouldn't have walked on it at all last night. I should have just let the stupid ostrich wander around our backyard, or find her own way back to the zoo.

Mom looked at me, concerned. She looked sad, too.

And all of a sudden, my head hurt. It felt like it was filled to the brim with things I couldn't say and lies and neverdos—Ethel, sneaking out of the house at night, my search for Jacob's ostrich, latent autism . . . so many secrets.

"You want some Tylenol for your foot?" Mom asked.

"Yes, please."

"And for breakfast—you want toast or an egg, maybe?"

"Toast would be good, thanks. Can I eat in here?"

"You feel bad enough to stay in bed?"

I shrugged.

"Well, I guess," she said. "Okay." She leaned over and kissed my forehead again before leaving the room.

I pulled the three-ring binder that held my *Peter Pan* script from my bedside table and turned to the page I was working on. I ran through the lines in my head and imagined each of the people in their places onstage. Performances were still three weeks away, but I wanted to be perfect. Jacob and I had rehearsal this afternoon. I'd have to tell Dorothy and Stephen I'd hurt my foot. I hoped they wouldn't be upset. It would make things a little trickier, but I knew I could still do this.

I was going over my lines at the part where I show Wendy how to fly when I heard Mom in the kitchen.

"No." She was calm but firm, and I knew she was saying it to Jacob. "No, no!" she said again. She was getting louder.

My stomach tightened.

"No, Jacob, stop," Mom said. "Stop!"

I could hear Jacob whining and kind of howling now, like an animal. He was upset. I pulled back the covers and put my feet on the floor.

"No, Jacob! That's enough," Mom said, louder.

I stood up and hobbled down the hall to the kitchen.

"Jacob! Jacob, no!" Mom yelled, and I made my way into the kitchen just in time to see my brother's flailing hands hit my mom right in the face. She cried out, and I felt the breath leave my body. Jacob howled, still flailing, but now he was flailing at the wall and the countertop. Food was flying from plates and the butter dish crashed to the floor. I didn't know what to do. My hands were shaking and my stomach felt sick.

Mom was trying to grab hold of my brother, but it was like trying to grab hold of something wild. Jacob was almost as big as Mom, and strong. It was hard for her to restrain Jacob and calm him down alone. And it was extra scary that Jacob could have another huge meltdown so soon.

Things were changing. Jacob was changing.

When Mom finally managed to contain my brother, she wrapped her arms around him, holding him still, pinning his arms to his sides, rocking back and forth in the middle of the kitchen. Both of them crying.

Mom pressed her cheek—red from where Jacob had hit her—against his back. They rocked and rocked and rocked. Jacob, sad and scared and lost, and my mom, trying to hold on to him.

I had to find that ostrich.

23

....

Pieces

DAD WAS UPSET. No, he was *angry*. Furious. Mom's face bruised where Jacob had hit her. Right across her cheekbone. Dad talked to Jacob. Loudly. But it didn't matter, really, because none of us could make it unhappen.

Jacob needed more than Mom could give him. So, that night, Mom and Dad decided they would hire an aide to help with Jacob two days a week, when Dad was at work. Jacob did better one-on-one with a steady stream of activities—drawing and working on projects, reading, playing games, that kind of stuff—and it was getting harder for Mom on her own all day long. Plus, it would be good to have extra help in case Jacob got too upset for Mom to handle.

Three days later, I walked in from helping our neighbor find his wallet to find Jacob sitting at the kitchen table, playing a board game with someone I didn't know.

"Oh, hi!" She looked up and smiled. "I'm Megan. I'm Dr. Kathy's assistant."

"Hi," I said. "I'm Olivia."

Dr. Kathy and Mom were in the living room, but Mom looked up when she heard me come in. I could tell she had been crying. I slipped off my shoes and stood quietly in the doorway. She wiped her eyes and came over to me.

"What's the matter?" I asked. It felt like someone had died. Someone, or something. Mom just shook her head and attempted a smile.

"I'm just trying to figure out how to handle things, Olivia. And it's hard." She glanced at Jacob.

"Harder than it was . . . before?" I asked.

She nodded.

"Is Jacob in trouble?"

"In trouble?"

"Because he hit you?"

"Oh, no!"

Mom reached out to me. She wrapped her arms around me and pulled me close. I rested my head on her shoulder. She smelled like soap and perfume.

"Jacob can't help the way he acts all the time," she said. Her voice was soft and muffled, heavy inside her own body and in my ear, which was pressed against her shoulder. "He didn't mean to hurt me, honey. He's just at a point where he can't express every-thing that's inside him, so sometimes it spills out in inappropriate ways. Imagine if you couldn't make the people who were supposed to love you the most understand the things you needed. Or if you didn't even know what you needed. That would be very hard, right?"

I watched my brother and Megan in the other room. Dr. Kathy was watching them, too. She got up and joined Jacob at the kitchen table, talking and smiling and asking him questions about the game he was playing.

I turned back to my mom. "So, how do we help Jacob?" I asked. "And how do we understand him if he can't tell us what he needs?"

Mom sighed. "Well, that's what Dr. Kathy and I were talking about," she said. "There are a lot of different options. So, we're just going to start exploring them until we find one that works best for Jacob, and for our family."

"What kinds of options?" I asked.

"Well, different kinds of therapy, some special tutoring, extra help here at home for Jacob—like your dad and I talked about."

"You mean an aide?"

"Mmm-hmm. Dr. Kathy is going to help us find someone who will be a good fit for Jacob. Someone who can help out from time to time. And we might think about some possible changes in environment, too."

I suddenly felt kind of dizzy.

An environment was a place where someone or something lived. When Phil said one of the animals at the zoo needed a change in environment, that usually meant they needed to be moved to a different pen for some reason or another. Sometimes, it was so we could clean the enclosure. Sometimes, it was so the animal could stretch its legs and move around in a bigger space.

I pulled out of Mom's arms and sat back so I could see her face. She looked tired, and sad. I was afraid to ask, but I had to know.

"What kind of change in environment? Is Jacob going to have to live somewhere else?"

"No!" Mom bit her lip and shook her head. "No," she said again, quieter. "We're going to do everything we can here at home before we consider anything more extreme. Dad and I have to talk more, and Dr. Kathy will help. We will explore everything, every tool that might be useful. Maybe even a therapy dog! Wouldn't that be fun?"

But I couldn't give Mom the answer she was looking for.

She continued, "As long as Jacob isn't intentionally violent— as long as he isn't trying to hurt me or you or Dad, and if we can try some new things that will make it easier for him and easier for all of us to work together and understand each other, your brother won't be going anywhere."

I looked over at Jacob, who was leaning over the board game in the kitchen. Did he know about all of this? Did he understand what was going on?

"Are you going to tell Jacob about everything?"

Mom nodded. "Of course. I don't know how much he'll understand, but Dad and I will definitely tell Jacob about everything we want to try."

"And what if *he* doesn't want to try?"

Mom didn't say anything, and when she did, her voice was low. She was trying not to cry.

"We're just going to take things one day at a time."

My heart thrummed in my ears. I felt sick.

Mom's voice was calm. But I knew she was only making it calm for me. I wanted to stomp my foot or scream or something, because this wasn't anything to be calm about. Not at all.

"We need to think about what's best for Jacob, and for our whole family. But please try not to worry. Everything is going to be okay."

I wanted to believe Mom, but it didn't feel like everything would be okay. It felt like everything was awful and only getting worse.

If my brother needed a change in environment, if he was sent away, then there was absolutely no going back. No matter what. Not for him, and not for me, either. My brother was still a part of this family, even when he frustrated me. He was a part of us as much as I was, and Mom and Dad. If he went somewhere else, were we even a family anymore? Or were we all just broken pieces?

I leaned into Mom's arms again so she couldn't see my tears.

24

....

Okay

THAT AFTERNOON I doubled my search for Jacob's ostrich.

I put big red *X*'s through the places Charlie and I had already looked on our map, and drew new places, too. It was now three sheets of paper taped together. I drew the street in front of our house. The park three blocks away. The post office five blocks past that. The corner market and gas station. I pulled my bike out of the shed because my foot was too tender to walk that far, and I pedaled to all the new places I'd drawn on the map.

I rode around the perimeter of the park and then made smaller and smaller circles through the grass, stopping every now and then to look carefully around tree stumps and playground equipment, too.

Nothing.

I rode to the post office, but it wasn't in their lost and found box, and when I talked to the clerk behind the counter, he hadn't seen Jacob's ostrich, either.

"Can you just check in the back room for me?" I asked. "Really quick? Or can I? It's super important."

"Miss, I'm very sorry, but I'm not authorized to allow you into the back room. Everything back there is property of the United States Postal Service, a branch of the US government."

"Even my brother's ostrich? If it's back there?"

The mail clerk rubbed his chin. "Well, no."

"Then can you look and see if it's back there? Just peek behind the boxes and check the corners?" I was nervous he'd say no again, but I had to ask.

"Peek behind the boxes and check the corners?" The clerk was looking at me like I was crazy. Maybe I was. But this was more important than he realized.

"Please?" I asked.

The clerk rubbed his chin again. "Well, shoot. All right." And he disappeared behind the door.

I could hear a bunch of muffled rustling. I closed my eyes and imagined Jacob's ostrich right where I wanted it to be. I imagined the clerk moving a few boxes here and there and checking the corners and then—

"I'm sorry, miss." I jumped and opened my eyes. "I didn't find any toys back there—ostriches or anything else." But he hadn't been gone very long. Maybe he hadn't looked hard enough.

"You looked behind the boxes?"

He nodded.

"And in the corners?"

The little metal bell over the door jingled as a new customer came in. The clerk smiled and looked relieved.

"I'm sorry," he said again. "But unless there's anything else I can help you with, I have another customer."

I tried not to show my disappointment. "No. That's all. Thank you for looking."

He nodded, and I limped back outside toward my bike.

After the post office, I rode to the gas station. The lady behind the counter hadn't seen Jacob's ostrich, either. I asked if I could search out by the pumps, and back behind the building where the air hose was coiled up and waiting to fill flat tires. She looked at me a little strangely but gave me a nod. With the money I'd earned from Mrs. Mackenelli, I bought a package of Starburst to reassure the gas-station attendant that I was a pretty normal person—normal people like Starburst—and after I looked and couldn't find anything, I got back on my bike and left.

I pedaled around town a little bit, keeping my eyes open. Maybe a clue would show up unexpectedly. But an hour later, there was still nothing. Not one single clue. I'd looked everywhere I could think of. I'd checked off every place on the map Charlie and I had made, and more. There was nowhere else to look.

I wished Charlie and I were talking so that I wasn't doing this alone. What would he say if he were here? What would he do?

What would Peter Pan do?

Peter Pan wouldn't stop looking until he found what he was looking for. Until he'd saved whoever it was that needed saving.

And just like that, I knew what I needed to do.

25

Working on Rhythm

"OLIVIA . . . *OLIVIA?* IT'S your line."

"Oh! Sorry. Um, where are we?" I couldn't focus. My mind was lining up every clue I'd collected. Every possible trail. Looking for a lead. Looking for Jacob's ostrich. But here onstage, Amelia—Wendy—was waiting for me to say my lines.

"I say, 'Mother and Father have decided it's time for me to grow up. This is my last night in the nursery!'" Amelia raised her eyebrows at me, waiting.

"Your last night? Absolutely not!" I said my line and stomped my foot on the stage. "Wendy, I will not allow it! You shall never grow up! You shall come with me to Neverland!"

"Neverland? What is Neverland?"

"Why, Neverland is the most wonderful place, full of pirates and mermaids and Indians and animals—beasts of all kinds. We have adventures every day, and no one ever tells us what to do, or where to go, or when to brush our teeth, or comb our hair, or go to school, or mind our manners, or eat our vegetables, and most importantly, there is no growing up allowed."

"No growing up?"

"Never."

I leapt across the stage and over to the giant window frame that stood in the middle. Fortunately, my foot was feeling much better. It had taken a week and a half, but the cut was healing over nicely. Before long there would just be a little scar, pink and shiny where the new skin would grow in.

But even though my foot was feeling better, and even though the bruise on Mom's face was gone, underneath those healed-over places, things still hurt a little. Maybe that was how it felt when someone you cared about hurt you.

"Where is this Neverland?" said Wendy.

"Second star to the right and straight on till morning." I pointed out over the audience. When people were actually sitting out there, I hoped they'd turn and look to see if there really was a star.

"But how shall we get there?" Amelia came to stand beside me just inside the window frame.

"We fly, of course!" And I'd show Wendy how.

I wore a harness under my costume, kind of like the harness rock climbers wear when they're climbing walls and mountains. But instead of attaching it to a rope, I'd be hooked to a very thin, very strong wire that wound up into a pulley system. A stagehand would sit on the other end of that pulley, raising and lowering me across the stage during all the flying scenes.

We weren't using the harness system yet, but on opening

night, after I said that line, I'd leap through the window and fly across the stage. It was one of my favorite parts in the whole play. Everyone knew there was flying in *Peter Pan*, but I had a feeling the audience wouldn't expect to see someone soar over the stage in a children's production.

Performances were just one week away, and I was trying not to be nervous, because things were going really well. Every part of the play was awesome. My lines. The sword fighting. Flying. I loved being the leader of the Lost Boys.

At home, with help twice a week from Ryan, Jacob's new aide, and a few new communicating and calming techniques that Dr. Kathy had suggested, things seemed a little better. But here at rehearsals was different. Jacob was actually doing well—better than I expected—as long as he could follow someone around onstage in each scene. He seemed to be enjoying himself, and he was more talkative than usual, too. The other kids didn't always know what to say to Jacob, but they didn't laugh as much anymore when he said weird things or acted a little strange.

He only has to say one line all on his own, without copying his twin.

"*Peter! You're back!*" That's what he says when I return to Neverland with Wendy, Michael, and John. But if something happens and Jacob can't play his part, one of the other kids can just as easily say that line. Or, if everyone forgets, and no one says it, it doesn't really matter that much.

Most of the cast knew their lines. Everyone knew where they were supposed to be, and where to stand. There was singing and dancing, and we all knew the choreography. We knew where and when to exit the stage, and when to come back on again. From now until opening night, we would be polishing scenes and working on pacing.

"We need to think about the rhythm, you guys!" Stephen was watching from the third row in the audience. "It's getting there, but I want you to think about how you're saying your lines, not just *what* you're saying. You need to think of this as a conversation. You're not just talking to each other onstage, you're talking to every person sitting out here." He stretched his arms to include the whole auditorium, and I felt the butterflies swirl around in my stomach.

"Amelia, can you take it from the top of that last scene?" Stephen looked at the script in his hand and shuffled his papers. "Take it from, 'Mothers are the most wonderful thing in the whole world!'"

Amelia nodded and sat down onstage. The Lost Boys resumed their places around her, some lying onstage, one resting his head on her shoulder, some sitting expectantly in front of her. Even John and Michael. They were all listening to Wendy remind them of what they'd forgotten.

"Mothers are the most wonderful thing in the whole world," Amelia said, clasping her hands in front of her and looking around at the boys.

In character as Peter Pan, I harrumphed and crossed my arms.

Being in Neverland makes everyone forget who they are or where they came from before. Except Wendy—she hadn't quite forgotten because in her heart, she did want to grow up . . . someday. Peter Pan never forgot, either—at least, he never forgot his mother, because she was the reason he had come to Neverland in the first place. She was the reason he never wanted to grow up. Because grown-ups forget what it's like to be a child.

Amelia kept going. "Mothers give you kisses and hugs and tell you bedtime stories. They tuck you in at night and greet you every morning. They wipe away your tears and soothe you when you're sick. They are the first people in the world to love you when you're born. And they love you exactly as you are—"

I jumped up and stomped across the stage, interrupting her story.

"Oh, really? Mothers love you exactly as you are?" I rolled my eyes and acted all tough, pretending I didn't need a mother, *or anyone* for that matter, when truthfully, I did. A lot. That was one of the reasons Peter invited Wendy to Neverland in the first place. And the audience knew it. "Mothers only want good boys and girls who never make mistakes or fly away! Why do you suppose any of you are here in the first place?"

I laughed at them as they went from enjoying Wendy's story to fearing the worst. Wendy stomped her foot and took control amid the rising panic of the Lost Boys, gathering them close and comforting them as a real mother would do. She glared at me as the Lost Boys sniffled and whimpered.

"Fine!" I said, waving my arms around. "Don't believe me! But one day you'll see! One day you'll fly back to your own house and your own window and there will be another boy sleeping in your bed! Your mother will have replaced you!" Then I stomped offstage as the Lost Boys erupted into fresh tears and wailing.

In the next scene, Wendy decides to return home with her brothers and take the Lost Boys with her. They make plans and pack their things, and I do some more stomping around and harrumphing, convinced of what they'll find. Warning them. And while they're busy getting ready, I fly back to Earth, back to my home and the window I flew out of years earlier to see my own mother. She's tucking children into bed. Other children. My siblings. The children I'm convinced she replaced me with. But my mother doesn't see me. She doesn't see that I've become Peter Pan. And just as I fly away toward Neverland, the audience sees my mother turn and look out the window at the empty night sky.

"Oh, Peter," she says, so sad. "Wherever have you gone? Come back to me . . ." But I never hear her and I never see, and I never know how much I'm wanted by the people who love me.

When we first acted out the scene in practice, I didn't want to do it. It felt out of place in such a happy, silly play about a boy who never grows up. It actually made me cry a little bit, though I tried not to let anyone see. But Dorothy explained that the scene was probably the most important one in the whole play. It shows the audience that Peter wants to be loved exactly as he is, more than anything in the world—even more than never growing up. It shows the audience that everyone makes mistakes, but that love never, ever gives up.

After that I decided I didn't want to take that scene out of the play after all. Instead, when we got to that scene and a real live audience was sitting out in all those chairs, I wasn't going to hide it if I started to cry. I wanted Charlie out there in that audience. I wanted to make things right with him. I needed him to know that I liked him exactly for who he was, and that I wasn't looking away.

After rehearsal, Jacob was in good spirits. Mom saw it, too.

"'Peter, you're back!' That's my line," he said to Mom on the ride home. He told her this after almost every rehearsal.

"It's a great line," she said.

"I like that I am in a play," said Jacob.

"Me, too!" Mom smiled. "Are you excited for opening night, Jacob?"

Jacob didn't answer.

"Or maybe a little nervous? It's perfectly okay if you are."

Still no response. It was raining and Jacob was busy pressing his fingers against the window, tracing the wavering trail of water droplets across the glass.

"How about you, Olivia? Are you nervous?"

"A little." I shrugged. "I just don't want to mess up."

"I think you'll be just fine. Better than fine. I think you'll be wonderful." Mom smiled and I knew she meant it. But I wasn't nervous for the reasons she thought I was. Being onstage and having people watch me say my lines, fly around, sing, dance, and pretend to be something that I wasn't was exciting. Because at least when I was onstage, everyone would know my pretending was on purpose. They would know I was someone else underneath the pretending—under the costume and stage makeup.

But in real life, all my pretending—that everything was fine, that I wasn't still looking for Jacob's ostrich, that I didn't know about latent autism—felt like a lie. And that made my stomach twist around in a way that being onstage never did. No one knew what I might be underneath all my neverdos. And I needed to keep it that way.

26

A Good Apology

A FEW DAYS later, I was eating breakfast, still nervous about opening night.

"Did you know the stirrup is the smallest bone in the human body?" Jacob asked.

He was sitting at the kitchen table, too, and Ryan sat beside him, flipping through the newspaper. When he found the funny pages, he pulled out the comics and handed them to my brother, who was waiting patiently, his hands folded in his lap.

I pushed a lonely Cheerio around my cereal bowl.

I'd heard Jacob's question, but I wasn't in the mood to answer. I was thinking about Charlie. He hadn't come around all week while I was working at the zoo. Not once. If he didn't show up today, I would go knock on his door until he answered.

"Did you know that, Olivia?" Jacob asked again. He didn't look at the comics. He was still waiting for me to answer.

"Did you know the stirrup is the smallest bone in the human body?" Jacob repeated his question.

"No, Jacob," I said. "I didn't know that." It was what he wanted me to say. It's what he always wanted me to say. I looked up from my cereal bowl.

Jacob smiled. "It is also known as the stapes," he said. "It is one of the three smallest bones in the human body. It is found deep inside the ear where the bone vibrates in response to sound."

"That's interesting," I said, but I didn't really mean it. I didn't care.

I picked up my bowl, dropped it in the sink, and went to my bedroom to change into the jeans and T-shirt I always wore when I worked at the zoo. I could feel Dad's eyes on my back, and Mom's, too. They could tell I was being quieter than usual, but nobody pressed it.

When I came back into the kitchen, I put on my shoes. "I'll be back after lunch," I said.

"Have a good morning, sweetheart." Mom kissed my forehead and stared into my eyes until I had to look away.

"Thanks," I mumbled. Then I slid open the porch door and walked through the backyard, down the minimal maintenance road toward the zoo.

Bridget was off today, so I was helping Phil. It was very, very quiet. Even the monkeys weren't chattering yet. Seeing no sign of Charlie only made things worse.

I was upset, and I was having trouble hiding it. Especially when I knocked over a bucket of grain by accident, spilling it everywhere.

Phil looked at me and raised his eyebrows. "Tough morning, eh?"

"Whatever," I said. I blinked hard as he handed me a broom. "Sorry."

"Don't worry about it," he said.

I started sweeping up the grain. When I couldn't take it any longer, I asked Phil the question I'd been wondering for more than a week. "Do you know where Charlie, Vera's son, is? I haven't seen him lately."

Phil stared at me for a minute and then shrugged. "Don't know," he said. "Is that what's eating you this morning? You and your boyfriend have a fight?" He grinned like he had it all figured out.

I felt my face heat up.

"What? No! He's not my *boyfriend*!" Charlie was my *friend*, and stupid Phil was just thinking up things that weren't true. Besides, it was none of his business. *1-2-3-4 in . . . 1-2-3-4 out . . .* "I just . . ." I took one more deep breath and let it out, nice and slow. "I said something to him last week, and I think I hurt his feelings. I just wanted to tell him I was sorry. But I haven't seen him around."

Phil looked at me, his face going serious and kind of soft around the eyes.

"Well then," he said. "That's different." He nodded. "That's brave."

"Brave?" It reminded me of what Mrs. Mackenelli had said about Mom. "How is that brave?"

He shrugged. "Trying to right a wrong is always brave."

I stared at him for a minute and then swept up the rest of the spilled grain.

As soon as I finished my work, I put away my tools and made my way to Charlie and Vera's trailer. I didn't know how to start. Apologies were hard. I thought I knew what I wanted to say, but now that I was standing at the bottom of Charlie's front steps, none of the words in my head felt right. But before I had time to sort out a few that did, Charlie opened the door.

"Hey, Olivia."

"Oh. Hi, Charlie," I said. "How'd you know it was me?"

"You were talking to yourself again. The windows are open."

"Oh."

"Everything okay? It sounded serious."

"Well, it is kind of serious. I think."

Charlie frowned. Already this wasn't going like I'd imagined.

"Not *serious*, serious . . ." I paused so I could gather my words. "More like *important*."

"Okay." Charlie waited.

"Um." I cleared my throat. "I'm sorry."

"You're sorry?"

"Yeah. You know, for *that thing* I said, before. When you were at my house. Remember?"

"I remember," he said.

Of course he did. I couldn't see his eyes, but his voice told me he was still hurt.

"So . . . yeah. I'm really sorry."

Charlie just stood there.

I rubbed my forehead. I needed to make him understand. I needed him to know I wanted to be his friend. No matter what.

"What I mean is, the stuff I said about wanting to be normal and wanting to have a more normal family, and normal things—that's true. But I didn't say it right. It's not what I meant *exactly*."

Charlie's eyebrows were scrunched again. He sat down on the top step, and I went up and sat down beside him.

"You know when Jacob said that thing about the leaves, when you were at my house? About green and chlorophyll and disguises?"

He nodded.

"Well, I think maybe people are like that, too." The words were just coming out of my mouth now, and I hadn't practiced any of them. "I think maybe my family is all kinds of colors. And you're all kinds of colors, and I'm all kinds of colors, too, and maybe everyone is. Like leaves. But we all wear green because that's the color that seems easiest for everyone to understand. That's normal. But maybe it's not real . . . It's sort of pretend, actually. Or a disguise. Like you said."

Charlie was listening with his whole self.

"So . . . I think everyone is a little bit not normal in one way or another. And maybe if we all just told each other the truth about that a little more, it might be easier to be all different kinds of colors."

I looked at Charlie, but I couldn't read his expression.

After a minute, he said, "So, what kinds of colors am I?" His voice was low and small. We were sitting very close now, and I could see my face reflected in his glasses. It was a good question, and I didn't need to think long before I knew the answer.

"Gold," I said. I took a deep breath. "And red and orange and blue and purple and pink, and *all of them*." My heart was pounding, but I didn't look away. I didn't move. Not even when Charlie leaned in like he was trying to feel the truth in my voice.

"Really?"

I looked at myself in his glasses, and then I closed my eyes so I could see—or not see—the world the way he did.

"Really," I said.

"Well, I think you're all the colors, too, Olivia."

I kept my eyes closed. I couldn't see a single thing. But inside I felt like an explosion of color.

27

Opening Night

AFTER CHARLIE AND I talked, we spent the whole afternoon looking for Jacob's ostrich. But we were still no closer to finding it than before.

For the rest of the week, I was even busier. Charlie and I searched for the ostrich every day after my work at the zoo and before rehearsal, but we still had nothing to show for it. It took everything I had to forget about searching in the evenings and just focus on being Peter Pan during our final rehearsals. There were costume checks and lighting cues to work out, and the final set pieces were moved into the theater. I got to practice flying for real in the harness, and the dress rehearsal went well. Everyone hit the right spots onstage and Jacob didn't melt down, or do anything too weird, or say anything he shouldn't. He remembered his one line, and Dorothy and Stephen stood up and clapped for us at the end.

We were ready. Tonight was opening night.

I wanted everything to be perfect. But I was extra nervous because Jacob's ostrich was still missing. All I could do now was concentrate, try my best, and hope that Jacob did the same.

The plan was to eat an early dinner and then head to the theater. But I wasn't very hungry. My stomach was too full of butterflies.

I had a lot to do before the show started, and I was excited to put on my costume and do my stage makeup once I got to the theater. Jacob was already wearing his costume. Since he was very particular about his clothes and getting dressed, Mom had talked to Stephen and Dorothy, and they agreed to let him put it on at home. All the Lost Boys in the play wore jeans with holes and T-shirts. The shirt was fine, but Jacob hated jeans. He never wore them.

"My pants are scratchy!" he moaned at the table. He flipped a piece of broccoli off his plate and onto the floor. "I don't like green!" He rocked back and forth and drummed on the table with his hands.

"Jacob," Mom said. She kept her voice very calm and low. "Jacob, I need you to take a deep breath and count with me. Okay?"

Jacob didn't look at her, he just plucked at his jeans and kept rocking and pushing broccoli around on his plate. But he counted and took deep breaths.

"One . . . two . . . three . . . four . . ." And then he let out a big breath and smiled. Just like that, it was over.

"Good job, Jacob," Mom said. Jacob smiled. Mom smiled. Then she looked at Dad. He smiled, too, and they both turned to look at me. Even though I hadn't found Jacob's ostrich, even though I was nervous, I smiled back. Then we quickly finished eating and raced to Tulsa for opening night.

Backstage, everyone was in various stages of getting ready.

Katie, the head of the costume department, tucked a strand of hair back under my cap, pinning it down with a bobby pin. My cap was brown and pointed, but made out of newspaper. You could even see the print coming through the brown paint. And it had a peacock feather stuck in it. Purple and blue and green. I had assumed my costume would be green and have tights and stuff. Like in the movie. But Dorothy wanted to do things differently. So, all of our costumes looked like a punk rock band of kids had spent the afternoon with a group of woodland creatures and traded clothes with each other. The Lost Boys wore jeans and T-shirts with holes in them, but then they had extra stuff, too. A vest made of pretend animal fur. A crown of pretend feathers. Gloves with pretend claws. That kind of stuff. It was pretty cool, actually. My costume was made out of felt leaves—brown and red and orange, all tied together with gold netting. I had a leather belt thing that was also a kind of holster for the fake sword I carried. On the bottom, I had on brown corduroy pants cut off just below the knee. And Chucks. Spray-painted gold. They reminded me of Charlie.

Once my hat was in place, I peeked out from behind the curtain. The theater was slowly filling with people of all ages. Ushers stood at the doors taking tickets and handing out programs and showing people to their seats. Excitement pulsed through the air like an electric current, bouncing from person to person.

After a few minutes, I found Charlie and Vera sitting stage right, halfway up the aisle. They looked excited, too. I would try to deliver my lines especially to Charlie. So he could see the play by the way I said things.

Eventually, I spotted Mom and Dad—three rows from the front, right in the center section. They were smiling and talking to each other, but they looked a little nervous. I hoped I would make them proud.

"All right, can I have everyone onstage, please?" Dorothy's voice pulled me from my thoughts as she called us all together for an opening night pep talk. I looked around for Jacob, who was standing on the other side of the stage. The makeup made his eyes look larger and darker than usual. All the Lost Boys wore hairstyles and makeup that made them look a little dirty and bedraggled. Like they played outside in the woods and never combed their hair or washed their faces.

As Dorothy talked, Jacob flapped his hands and plucked at his jeans.

"This is it!" she said. "Now, you've all worked really hard these past few weeks, and Stephen and I are so proud of this play."

"That's right," Stephen chimed in. "So, don't worry if someone drops a line or misses a step. Just keep going. Now go out there and have fun! Break a leg, everyone!"

"Places, please! Places," called the stage manager.

Everyone rushed to get into their places for act 1, scene 1, and

I ran over to my brother as quickly as I could. "Break a leg, Jacob!" I whispered.

"Break a leg, Jacob!" he repeated.

I did my best to breathe.

Then the lights in the theater dimmed, the auditorium grew very quiet, and the curtain lifted on the opening scene.

The play was starting.

"But it isn't fair!" Wendy shouted, stomping her foot. "I don't want to grow up!"

"Everyone grows up," insisted her father, Mr. Darling, matter-of-factly.

"It's a rule for being a person," agreed Mrs. Darling.

I watched from the stage left wings, my stomach turning and knotting. The audience was quiet, listening and taking it all in.

This was it. This was what I'd been waiting for. I ran my fingers over the beautiful feather in my newspaper cap. I loved my costume. I loved the feel of the stage under my feet. The gloss of the wood. The heat of the stage lights that almost blinded me to the audience. I loved the murmur of voices and the feeling that I was doing something special.

The play had six acts, and by the time we got to number five—the part where Captain Hook and I have a sword fight—I felt like maybe I really could fly. My insides were full of air and light. This was my favorite scene. The one where I rescue everyone—Wendy, Michael, John, and the Lost Boys—after they all get captured by Hook.

The stage lights were hot, and sweat trickled down my back where my harness was buckled around my waist. I was breathless from singing and dancing and from flying across the stage. I'd only messed up my lines once. Just a tiny bit, and I don't think anyone really noticed.

Everyone onstage was tied up. Wendy was on the plank with Captain Hook's sword at her back.

"En garde, you cowardly codfish!" I shouted, flying across the stage with my harness and invisible wire, my sword pointed straight at Captain Hook.

"Codfish? Codfish!" Hook hated being insulted. He whirled around, our swords met, and the fight was on. We'd practiced this scene until we could do it anywhere, anytime. *Right foot forward, right arm back, swing, duck, swing again. Dodge, slash left, then slash right, and swords meet overhead.* Across the stage we went, turning and spinning, shouting insults at each other and both of us trying to beat the other with our fancy swordsmanship. Of course, Peter had the advantage because he could fly.

"Are you afraid, boy?" Hook jeered as I flew out of reach again. "Who is the coward now? I, at least, keep both feet on the ground! But you! Look at you, always flying away!"

"Coward? I am no coward!" Peter hated being insulted as

much as Hook. I landed and planted both feet firmly on the stage. "You want to fight? Fine! Let's fight. No flying!"

"No flying?" Hook looked at the audience with a wicked grin.

"No flying!" I shouted. "I give you my word! And my word is as good as my life."

Hook laughed a sinister laugh and lunged as we fought across the stage again. But this time there was no flying. And by the time Hook pinned me to the ground, I was truly out of breath.

"Wait!" Wendy screamed as the evil captain raised his sword. But I shook my head at her.

"It's okay, Wendy," I said. The audience was completely silent. "To die will be an awfully big adventure!"

Hook plunged his sword. But just before it touched me, Tinker Bell—a bright flickering light rather than a real person—swept in across the stage. When everyone else was focused on her flicker and Hook was distracted, I wiggled out of his grasp. Again he swept with his sword and missed. He lunged, and tripped, and before the audience knew what was happening, Hook tumbled overboard off the set with a loud "Arrrrrrrrrggghhhhhh" and disappeared from view into the waves and the mouth of the waiting Tick-Tock Croc below—through a trapdoor in the stage.

Silence hung over the stage for just a moment as the Lost Boys and Wendy, Michael, and John collected their breath for a mighty cheer.

And then my brother fell to his knees.

"My pants are scratchyyyyyy!" Jacob cried out, long and loud into the quiet auditorium.

No one said a word. Everyone onstage and everyone in the audience was silent, trying to understand. And then someone in the back snickered. And then someone else. And then lots of people were laughing.

I couldn't breathe.

All of the buildup and the hard work, every line I'd remembered, every step and cue, every exit and entrance onstage, every part every character had played so perfectly to get us to this moment came crashing to a halt. The laughing continued and everyone forgot all about Peter Pan, and the Lost Boys, and Wendy, and Hook, and the pirates, and never growing up. They all laughed at my brother, rocking back and forth onstage, desperately scratching and plucking at his pants.

And then, slowly, they realized it wasn't part of the play.

Slowly, the laughing stopped.

I wanted to fall through the trapdoor with Hook and stay there until it was over. I wanted to shut my eyes and pretend it was a bad dream. I wanted to jump off the stage and fly away on my invisible wire. But I didn't do any of those things. I just stood there and stared at my brother. And then I looked into the audience at Dad and Mom—half sitting, half standing, their eyes wide, not knowing what to do or how to help.

I looked into the wings. Even Dorothy stood as still as a statue.

I didn't see Stephen anywhere. I was the only one who could help.

But I didn't want to.

I didn't want to be Olivia Grant.

I didn't want to be the sister of the strange Lost Boy onstage, crying and scratching and rocking back and forth.

Right now I was Peter Pan. I wanted to have sword fights and adventures and fly and be the hero.

So, I didn't move a muscle. Not even when Jacob looked at me. When he met my gaze for the briefest moment—something he almost never did. I just let him cry and wail all alone onstage.

And then the lights came on, and the curtain came down.

For a minute, everything was total confusion. The audience started talking and laughing, trying to figure out what was going on. Everyone onstage stayed in their places, trying to figure out what to do next.

Suddenly Mom and Dad were backstage with Jacob, leading him into the wings and out of view. I kept trying to shake the look he'd given me out of my head. The look that said he was afraid and confused and sorry and knew he'd ruined everything. A look I had pretended to ignore as I stood perfectly still onstage and did nothing to help.

And now what? Was the play ruined? I had no idea what I was supposed to do.

Some of the other cast members started moving around, but all I could do was stand in place. I was frozen.

A few minutes later, Dorothy called us all together onstage again and announced that we'd be picking up right where we left off. The stage manager called places again, and on the other side of the curtain we heard Stephen speak.

"Ladies and gentlemen! We apologize for the brief interruption."

I listened as Stephen turned everything around with just a few words. "We trust you are ready to return to Neverland, where our brave hero, Peter Pan, has just saved the day!"

Everyone clapped, and the curtain rose again as the audience's attention turned to me, standing in the spotlight.

I tried to look for my parents, but the glare was too bright; I couldn't see anything.

I wanted to scream at everyone to stop. I hadn't saved the day. I hadn't saved anything or anyone and I never would. I wasn't a hero. And I was most definitely not brave.

But I was playing the role of Peter Pan, so I did the only thing I could think of. I raised my fist in the air and crowed the best crow I could manage. And I cheered, too. Because that was my job, and I'd already let enough people down.

Then I said my line and led the Lost Boys—minus Jacob—in a celebratory chorus.

"Hip, hip, hooray! Hip, hip, hooray! Hip, hip, hooray!" we all shouted.

But the whole thing felt like one big lie.

Neverdo List, Entry #5

1. Never leave Jacob alone onstage when he needs me.

28

....

Ruined

AFTER OPENING NIGHT, Jacob didn't rejoin the show. Mom and Dad sat me down that night and explained that the stress of being onstage, in front of an audience, was too much for Jacob. I had been right. The very thing I'd been afraid of happening had happened, just like I'd predicted it would. But I didn't feel good about it.

We'd all been so excited about *Peter Pan* that we had pretended. We had pretended at dinner on opening night, and we had pretended on the way to Tulsa. We had pretended once we got there and went off to get ready, too. We'd pretended that Jacob was okay. Because sometimes, when you want something so much, you let yourself pretend it's true.

But pretending doesn't make real things less real—it just covers them up for a little while. And when they get too real to be covered up anymore, those real things are just as they always were. Except they feel harder to deal with than you remember.

I wasn't happy that Jacob wouldn't be rejoining the play, but it was a relief not to have to worry about him after that. I could concentrate better. Performing was easier once he was out of the show.

But it didn't feel quite as fun.

And then, just like that, it was Thursday. *Peter Pan* was over. We'd performed six shows in six days. It was a lot, but it had mostly been great. Dorothy and Stephen had even let me keep my costume. The newspaper cap with its peacock feather, the gold netting laced with felt leaves, the gold painted shoes, my sword and scabbard. All of it. I couldn't wait to show Charlie.

"So, are you sad the play is done? I would be. You did so great, but I really think the final show was your best."

Charlie had come to two of the five performances. Now, I was back at the zoo, and he was helping me with my remaining Responsibility Hours. It was late July and I had just one week left at the zoo.

His cane swept the ground in front of us, rattling grass and weeds as I raked up hay in the donkey cage. Puffs of milkweed seeds flew up in little clouds whenever we brushed by them.

"Thanks," I said. "But anything would have been better than opening night."

"Not true! I think it was really brave the way you kept going after Jacob fell apart up there!"

Brave? Was he serious?

"Charlie, I just stood there. Jacob was having a meltdown. He was all alone and upset and scared, and I didn't do anything to help him. That wasn't brave. It was cowardly and selfish."

"Well, didn't everyone just stand there for a minute or two?"

"Yes, but I'm his sister. I was the one person who could have helped, and I didn't."

"So . . . why didn't you?"

"I don't know," I said softly. But that wasn't the whole truth. "I guess part of me didn't want to." It felt strange to admit it out loud. And I was worried what Charlie would think. "Wow. That sounds really mean, doesn't it?"

Charlie was quiet for a minute.

"Just . . . honest, I guess," he said. "And you help Jacob a lot. You're always there to answer his questions and fix stuff that he can't do on his own. I've heard how you talk to him. But I don't think it's, like, your *job*. You know? You can't do everything for him all the time. Even when you think you should help, maybe it's okay if, once in a while, you don't."

"But families take care of each other! That's like, *Rule Number One!*"

Charlie laughed. "Trust me, I know that better than a lot of people," he said. "But it's okay to let other people help, too. And other people did!"

I sighed. "I guess so."

"Were your parents mad you didn't do something onstage?"

"No. They didn't even seem to think I should have."

"See?" Charlie smiled. "Plus, maybe Jacob needs to learn to help himself sometimes, too."

"He does help himself. He's actually really independent." I suddenly felt kind of defensive.

Charlie stopped and faced me.

"Olivia, how do you think I learned to use a cane and get around after I lost my eyesight?"

"Um, I don't know."

"I practiced. A lot. And sometimes it was super scary. But if my mom hadn't let me go out and find my way around new places, I'd still be sitting in our trailer, by myself, in the dark."

"So, you're saying I should just let Jacob melt down and not do anything?" I folded my arms across my chest.

"No." Charlie sighed. "I just think he can probably do more than you realize. So, give yourself a break."

I tried not to roll my eyes.

After we finished at the zoo, Charlie and I walked to my house. Mom met us at the door when we got there.

"Hi, Mom. We were just—" The look on her face stopped me. "What's wrong?"

"Honey, listen . . ."

I could hear the concern in her voice. I wondered if Charlie could hear it, too.

"Olivia, after you left, Jacob disappeared for just a few minutes. I found him in your room . . ." She trailed off and her voice got very gentle. "He didn't mean to, honey . . . He doesn't understand . . ."

A kind of hollowness opened up inside me, and I pushed past her. I ran down the hall and into my room.

My costume lay in a pile on the floor.

In dozens and dozens of pieces.

It had been hanging up. On display. So I could look at it whenever I wanted. So Charlie could feel it. Now it was completely ruined. Fragments of red and orange and brown leaves, and slivers of shredded gold netting lay scattered across the rug. The newspaper hat was just a pile of ripped brown paper strips.

Big things made small.

I knelt down on the floor. Something hot was rising from that hollow place in the pit of my stomach. I looked around my room, trying to catch my breath.

Mom appeared in the doorway and Charlie stood beside her. She didn't say anything for a minute; she just looked at me, and then she reached out with both arms. But I didn't want to be hugged. I didn't want to be touched.

"I am so sorry, honey. I'm so, so sorry. How can I help? We could try to glue your hat back together?" Her eyes were swimming as she started to pick up the pieces.

I held out my hands, and she emptied bits of feather into my palms. Jacob had even cut up the peacock feather that had been attached to my hat. The pieces were so light they felt almost invisible. But they were heavy, too. I could hardly hold them in my hands.

"I'm really sorry, Olivia," Charlie said quietly.

"It's ruined," I whispered. "Jacob ruins *everything*."

It felt good to say it.

"I wanted to show you, Charlie." My words got tight, and I had to clear my throat a couple of times to get them all the way out. "I wanted you to be able to feel it and, like, really *know* my costume. But there's nothing to show you now."

Charlie just lowered his head. Like he didn't know what to say or do next. Mom sighed.

"I'll walk back with you," I said. And I took Charlie by the hand and left without saying another word to my mom. If I said or did anything else, I'd have to fill my entire notebook with neverdos.

Charlie and I didn't say a word all the way back to the zoo. Not one word. The quiet was so loud it hurt my ears.

When we got to the gate, we stopped, but instead of going inside, Charlie held my hand and squeezed tight. And he didn't let go.

"I'm sorry, Olivia," he said. I could hear sadness in his voice. He took a breath, like he was trying to find words. "Just don't be too mad at your brother. Okay? Promise?"

But I couldn't. I couldn't promise him anything like that. So, I lied.

"Okay. I promise."

Then I walked slowly all the way home, kicking at rocks and twigs as I went.

29

Solar Flare Words

WHEN I GOT home, my costume was right where I'd left it. A pile of fabric scraps. Gold and brown and red and orange on my bedroom floor. It looked even more ragged and broken now.

I folded my legs under me and sat, staring at it. So much mad was tornado-ing around inside me, I felt like I could spontaneously combust at any moment. That costume had been special. It was the thing that made me something else. Some*one* else.

What had Jacob even been doing? Why had he cut it into pieces? What part of my costume had made things feel too big for him? I was so mad at Jacob, but I was mad at myself, too. I never should have taken it home. It was too special. I should have known Jacob would just ruin it like he ruined everything. Maybe he was punishing me for not doing anything to help him onstage? Maybe I deserved it. Was this Jacob's way of telling me that some part of this had been my fault?

I ran my fingers over the scraps of fabric. And then tears started running down my face.

Suddenly my bedroom door opened. My brother walked in—without even knocking, without being told he could enter. He had never done that before.

"Jacob! What are you doing in here? Get out of my room!" I jumped to my feet, brushing the tears from my cheeks.

He just stood there in the middle of my room, not looking at me, rocking back and forth, tugging on his shirtsleeves.

"That is ruined," he said, pointing to what used to be my costume.

"I know," I said. My voice sounded hard as glass. "You cut it up, Jacob. *You* ruined it!"

Jacob started laughing. But it wasn't the kind of laughing you do when you're happy. It was the kind of laugh that happens when you're scared and don't know what to do or how to make things better. Like shivering. You can't control it.

"You ruin *everything*!" I shouted. Tears were streaming down my face. My heart was pounding. "I hate you. I. Hate. You!" The words flew out like a solar flare. Blazing. The speed of light. I couldn't have stopped them if I'd wanted to.

Mom ran into the room. "What's going on?"

"I cut it up," Jacob said. "I cut it up. I cut it up. I cut it up." And he laughed again. But then he slapped himself in the face with the palm of his hand. Hard. So hard it left a mark. I gasped and jumped away from him.

He'd never done that before, either.

"Oh! Oh, Jacob," said Mom, reaching for him before he could do it again.

"I cut it up," he said again. He was staring over my shoulder into space and flapping his hands like he was trying to fly away. Away from me and away from the mess he'd made.

I stood there in the middle of my room, watching and listening while Mom talked to Jacob. Quiet, soft words. Calm words. Safe, protecting, helping words. Then she led him out of my room and closed the door behind her.

I sat frozen for a minute. I'd never told anyone I hated them before. Not ever. Mom and Dad were pretty serious about our words. "Hate" was one we absolutely never used.

"Saying you hate someone is as bad as saying you wish they'd never been born," Dad had told me. And I had just used that terrible word on my brother. I felt exactly like the pile of fabric scraps on my bedroom floor. Ragged and ruined.

I stood up and looked around my room. Before I could stop myself, I picked up my copy of *Peter Pan* from where it was sitting on my nightstand and threw it. Hard. It arced across the room and hit the wall in a flutter of pages, falling to the floor like a lifeless bird.

With a single sweep of my arm, I brushed a pile of papers off my desk, then tipped over the desk chair.

With everything I tore apart, something inside of me cracked a little more.

I pulled open my dresser drawers, tearing clothes from them and throwing them across the room until jeans and T-shirts, socks and underwear carpeted the floor around me.

I threw my pillow as hard as I could against my bedroom door, knocking a nearby picture off its hook and to the floor.

I was breathless and shaking. I stopped and looked around at the mess I'd made. My room didn't look like my room anymore.

I curled up on my bed and pulled the covers over my head until everything was dark and muffled.

I screamed.

And cried.

Solar flare after solar flare until I burned out. No one even came in to check on me.

When I woke up later, I thought I'd gone blind for a minute. My eyes were open, but I couldn't see anything.

After I realized I'd fallen asleep under the covers, I pulled them off my head and rolled over. My room was dark. I'd slept all afternoon and into the evening. The glowing numbers on my clock read 9:43 p.m. No one had woken me for dinner.

There was a heavy weight in the pit of my stomach. The memory of my words rushed out at me. I went over and over them the way you examine your knee after you've fallen on the pavement—searching for evidence to justify the pain, trying to assess how bad the damage really was.

This was bad.

I felt sick.

I pulled my knees to my chest in the dark and held myself there, not even daring to imagine how many things I'd have to write on my neverdo list now. Too many to count. They all blended together.

Latent autism.

I looked around my shadowy bedroom and then switched on my lamp. My desk chair was on the floor, and clothes and papers were strewn everywhere. My room was a complete disaster. I was already acting more like Jacob than myself.

This mess was the final proof.

30

Speaking Love

SOMETIME LATER, I fell asleep again, and when I woke up, it was the middle of the night. I rolled over, and my notebook of neverdos slid off the bed and hit the floor. I peered down to look at some of the things I'd written for a moment, but the whole thing felt pointless. The list wasn't working. I couldn't stop doing the things I was supposed to never do. I couldn't avoid being whatever I was becoming.

I got up to go to the bathroom, but something caught my eye and I looked out the window. Flashing red and blue lights cast their shine on the lawn.

Why were the police here?

I crept to my bedroom door and opened it quietly. Voices I didn't recognize and words and emotions poured in. Fear. Worry. Uncertainty. A dark wave rolled around in my stomach. What was going on?

I walked slowly down the hall toward the living room. Mom was on the couch. Her face was pinched and white. She looked up, and when she saw me, she held out her hand. Dad was standing off to one side, his arms crossed over his chest, his face twisted.

"What's the matter?" I whispered. But my voice didn't even sound like mine. There were two police officers in the living room. And just having them there, *in my living room*, made me feel like something horrible was going on. Could you go to jail for screaming terrible words at your brother?

"Jacob is gone," Mom said, her voice cracking.

"*Gone*?" The floor heaved. "What do you mean?"

"He ran away. He left the house sometime during the night."

"What do you mean? Where did he go?"

"That's what we're trying to figure out," one of the police officers said.

Guilt washed over me. This was my fault. But . . . he had to come back. Didn't he?

"This is Officer Blakeman and Officer Holtz," Dad introduced me to the officers. "They're heading up a search team so we can try to find Jacob." Officer Holtz smiled at me, but her eyes were serious.

"Hi," I said quietly.

The officers were here because of me. I glanced at Officer Blakeman. And then at Mom and Dad.

I hadn't done a single thing to help Jacob onstage opening night. Maybe this was my chance to make it right.

"My brother and I had a fight," I said. My voice was shaky. I stood in front of Officer Holtz, and she raised her eyebrows.

"Okay. Can you tell me what happened?"

I glanced at Mom. She'd come into my room when I was upset earlier, but I don't think she'd heard exactly what I'd said.

"Jacob cut up my Peter Pan costume," I said. "It was really special. I was coming home with my friend Charlie, because I wanted to show it to him." I was trying very hard to be brave and responsible. I wanted Mom and Dad to know I could handle difficult things, difficult conversations. But I was scared of what they would think when I told them the truth. They would be so disappointed in me. And that was worse than them being mad.

Officer Holtz smiled and pulled a notebook out of her pocket. "Let's sit down," she said. She sat at the kitchen table and patted a chair beside her. I sat, too, and folded my hands tight in my lap. She nodded at me to continue.

"When I got home with Charlie, I ran into my room and saw that my costume had been cut up into many, many little pieces. Jacob had cut it up."

"Do you know why he would do that?" Officer Holtz asked.

"He does that sometimes," I said. "It's like he's trying to make things that are big in his head small—so he can understand them better or something. I don't know why it had to be my costume, though."

Mom and Dad were listening, too. I had everyone's full attention.

I continued. "I was really upset so I left the house. When I got back, Jacob just barged into my room and started laughing and saying that he had cut it up. And I yelled at him." I stared at my hands in my lap. "I told him that he ruined everything. And . . . and . . . that I hated him."

I wanted to look at Mom and Dad, but I was too afraid of what I'd see in their faces. Now they knew that Jacob had run away because of me. This was my fault.

I was to blame.

No one said anything at first. No one sighed or muttered a single word under their breath.

Finally, Officer Holtz spoke. "Anything else?" She was holding her pen like she was waiting for more.

I shook my head and looked up. My parents just held hands on the couch. Their faces were incredibly sad.

"Can you think of anywhere he might be?" Officer Holtz asked. "Was there anything you said that might have led him to go somewhere specific?"

"I don't think so. I didn't say anything else."

The officer nodded and tucked her notebook into her back pocket.

"I'm sorry," I whispered. "Am I in trouble?"

Officer Holtz shook her head and reached over to squeeze my shoulder. "No. Officer Blakeman and I are here to help. Okay?"

"Okay," I said. But it didn't make me feel any better.

I wished Jacob was just asleep in his own bed. That he'd gone to sleep knowing I probably didn't mean what I said and that we'd talk about it in the morning, because that's what an older brother should do. But instead, my brother had run away in the middle of the night, and now there were police officers in my living room.

I was struggling not to cry.

Officer Holtz squeezed my shoulder again. "It's okay," she said. "If you remember anything else that might be helpful, you can let me know, okay?"

I nodded. "I could help you search?" I said.

Officer Holtz gave a small smile.

"I think you'd better let us have a go first," said Office Blakeman.

Dad came over and wrapped his arms around me. He kissed the top of my head. I closed my eyes and hugged him back. Mom sat on the couch with her head in her hands.

"It's okay, honey," Dad said. "We trust the officers to know what they're doing. And you've already been a big help. Thank you for being so honest."

I felt even sicker than before.

More police officers came and went as morning arrived. Mrs. Mackenelli walked over from across the street to find out what was going on, and then she sat with Mom for a while.

I called Vera to let her know what had happened, and to tell her I wouldn't be able to come to the zoo that morning.

"Oh, Olivia! I'm so sorry! Are you okay? How are your parents?" I could hear her concern through the phone.

"We're all okay, I guess, just very worried. But the police are looking for him."

"Should I let Charlie know?" Vera asked. "Or would you rather talk to him yourself? He's right here . . ."

I didn't want to talk to Charlie. He'd warned me. He'd told me not to get too mad at Jacob, and I had anyway. "Um, you can let him know," I said. "I'll talk to him later."

"Okay. Take care, Olivia. Tell your folks I'm here if they need anything."

"I will," I said. "Thanks."

I wanted to help, too, but I didn't know what to do, so I tried to remember everything I could about Jacob. One by one things rushed in.

The way he asked us questions all the time.

How he shared interesting facts.

How he was always careful to bring his dishes to the sink for Mom.

The way he'd drawn that ostrich picture for me.

The way he'd smiled at me onstage, as if he knew I was nervous.

The way he said my name. "*Ol-i-vi-a.*" Carefully. Exactly.

The way he put things together in very specific ways. Puzzles. Games. Patterns. He knew how things went together and came apart better than I did.

And then I remembered how he'd banged his head against the wall after he'd thrown the glass of milk. How he'd stood in the middle of my room and slapped himself after cutting up my costume. Had he been showing me he was upset? Or was he trying to tell me he knew what he'd done and that he wished he hadn't? Maybe he was trying to tell me that he was sorry.

What would that feel like—to have a thought or a feeling and not be able to communicate it? If I were my brother, would I be able to use words the way I wanted? Would they make sense?

I tried to picture Jacob and me, if we switched places. And I knew, even if I couldn't use the right words to tell him, even if I didn't know how to make him understand, I'd still want him to find me, if he could. More than anything. Even if something he'd said was the reason I'd run away in the first place. I'd want him to come for me, searching and never stopping, until I was home. Until I wasn't lost anymore. Until I was found and loved.

"I can find him," I said.

No one heard me.

Officer Holtz was talking to Dad and listening to her radio. Mrs. Mackenelli was talking to Mom. A couple other neighbors who'd come over were standing around talking to each other. So, I slipped my hand into Dad's and said it again, a little louder.

"I can find him."

Mom looked up, and Dad looked down at me, and then Officer Holtz looked at me, too.

"I'll find him," I said. And this time, it was a promise I made to my brother.

31

Lost Boy

THE POLICE HAD been searching for five hours.

Mostly they were looking behind the house where the state park met our backyard. The minimal maintenance road ran through that land until it got to the zoo, and then after the zoo it came to a cell tower. But besides that, there wasn't much out there. Just a lot of open space, and woods, and swamps, and hills, and many places a person could hide.

I had to join the search.

I tied my shoelaces into double knots. This was bigger than missing eyeglasses, or a missing wallet, or a ring, or a pet. Bigger than Jacob's ostrich.

"Sweetheart," Dad said as he sat down beside me on the bench by the door as I got ready to go. "I know you really want to help, but Officer Holtz thinks it would be a good idea if you stayed here. So do Mom and I."

"What?" I looked at him. "No!"

"Olivia, in cases like these, the family's involvement in searching often makes it more difficult for us to find a loved one," said Officer Holtz. "Important things can be missed and new complications can arise. We can't afford that now. Every minute counts."

"You don't understand. I have to go out and look for Jacob! I can find him! I know I can!"

"Olivia, I know you are extraordinarily good at finding things," said Dad. "But we need to let the experts do their job here."

"Dad, please! I—"

"We don't want to have to worry about you, too, Olivia," said Mom. She walked over to me and held my hand.

"We will *find* Jacob. We *will*." Dad said it twice, like he was trying to convince himself. "We just don't think you going out there is the best idea."

I shook off Mom's hand and stood up.

"Just listen to me. *Please*. Jacob is my brother, and he is out there right now waiting for me to come look for him. I have to find him. It's what I'd want him to do if it were me out there somewhere." Suddenly there was a lump growing in the back of my throat. "He is out there *because of me*. I can't stay here and let everyone else go out and look for Jacob when it's all my fault he's gone to begin with."

Dad stared at me for a minute, and then his eyes filled with tears. He wrapped his arms around me and hugged me so tight I almost couldn't breathe. But I wasn't finished yet. I pulled out of Dad's hug.

"Please, Officer Holtz?"

She looked over at my parents, then back at me.

"I can't just stay here," I said firmly. "I am a finder of lost things. I know I can find Jacob." I looked her in the eyes, begging her to let me do this.

She didn't get it.

Maybe she never would. Maybe no one would. But I couldn't watch Jacob disappear and never come back, like his toy ostrich. I couldn't just stand here, drawing maps and gathering pretend clues, while everyone else did what they were supposed to do.

"Sweetheart, it's not your job to find your brother," my mom said gently. Her words reminded me of what Charlie had said. And she was right. Maybe it wasn't my *job* to take care of Jacob. But I wanted to. This was one thing I had to do. So what if Jacob wasn't normal. Neither was I. Neither was anyone. And, yeah, sometimes things were hard. But Jacob was still my brother. And if I could do anything to help find him, I needed to do it.

"Look," I said, turning back to Officer Holtz. "I'm small. I can fit into small places." I crouched down and squished myself into a ball so she could see just how small I could get. "And I'm tough! I can walk and walk and walk, and I won't get tired. Plus, I'm not afraid of the dark, or of strange animals! I work at the zoo." I took a breath. "I notice things other people miss—that's what makes me such a great finder. You need me! And I—"

But Officer Holtz held up her hand, cutting me off. "What

makes you so certain you can find him?" She was still skeptical. She didn't want me going out there.

"It's true. Olivia is really good at finding things," Dad said. He glanced over at Mom. "Extraordinarily good. But more importantly, you said yourself that every minute counts."

Officer Holtz nodded.

"Well, every minute that passes is one minute closer to dark." Dad's voice got tight. "I think it's wise to use every resource we have at our disposal. Including Olivia."

Mom stood up and came to stand beside him.

Dad's argument sounded logical, and Officer Holtz must have thought so, too, because she looked at me and sighed. But she nodded, and Officer Holtz, Mom, Dad, and I all set off down the road.

When we met up with the police officer who was stationed at the search party's meeting point, I couldn't believe how many people were there to help. Most of them were officers and volunteers with training in this kind of thing. Mom's face was white and her eyes were wide. Dad wrapped his arm around her. They seemed to hold each other up. When Dad held out an arm for me, I sandwiched myself between them and held on tight as Officer Holtz explained how this was going to work.

"You will each get a whistle," she said, handing them out to the three of us. Each one dangled on the end of a white cord like a necklace, and we hung them around our necks. "If you find anything,

anything at all, a piece of fabric, an article of clothing, a footprint, a piece of hair, blood"—Mom squeezed my hand just for a second—"blow your whistle and keep blowing it until we can locate you. One of the officers will join you as quickly as possible and follow up on whatever it is you find."

I looked at everyone stretched across the tall grass. I didn't know them, but I knew they were here to help. They cared about my family. A lump rose in the back of my throat, and I swallowed hard.

"When it's time to start or stop, you'll hear an air horn," continued Officer Holtz. "Three blasts, a brief pause, and then three more."

We all nodded, understanding what we needed to do. And then we started walking.

We maintained ten-foot gaps of space between each person. As we walked through the grass and underbrush, we covered every inch of ground with our eyes and our feet. There was nowhere a thirteen-year-old boy could hide that we wouldn't see.

"Jacob! Jacob!" All down the line, the search party called his name. "Jacob!"

Mom walked beside me, ten feet away, pushing grass aside with her feet as she went, walking around trees and fallen logs, peering under thick brush.

I listened. I really truly listened for my brother. Not with my ears, but with everything I was. I gathered everything I knew about him—his habits, things and places that made him feel safe—and lined it all up in my mind.

Jacob hated wearing wet clothes. He would try to stay dry, so maybe we didn't have to worry about wet, swampy areas so much.

Jacob liked to be in small, safe places. We might need to look extra carefully for any kinds of holes or heavy underbrush or over-turned logs that could make for a shelter or cave he might want to hide in.

Jacob didn't like heights, so we probably didn't have to be nervous about him climbing trees.

I thought and thought. Each piece of information—a clue. Something that could help with the search.

It would be okay. I was extraordinarily good at finding things.

So, I added my voice to the line, calling my brother's name.

"Jacob! Jacob!" *It's me, Olivia. I'm here. I'm looking for you. And I'm sorry. I really am. Jacob, I can't remember the way. Can you take me home now?* "Jacob! Jacob! Jacob!" I called for my brother. Speaking love to him. Hoping he could understand.

We walked for hours. Eventually I lost track of time.

We walked through low land and mud swaths that smelled like decaying plants and buzzed with flies. We walked through grasses and weeds thick with burrs and thistles that stuck on our clothes and skin. We walked through underbrush so heavy I actually got down on my hands and knees and crawled through it, just like I told Officer Holtz I could.

We walked until the skin on my heels had been rubbed raw. Even when a branch whipped back and caught me in the face, I kept going. I was hot and burned from the blazing late afternoon sun, and horseflies buzzed around us, biting when they landed. But I didn't complain. I didn't cry. And I wouldn't stop. Not until we found Jacob.

And then, just before dark, someone started blowing an air horn.

Bwaaaa—bwaaaa—bwaaaa! Three short blasts. A pause. And then three more. *Bwaaaa—bwaaaa—bwaaaa!*

Everyone stopped. A woman in uniform next to Mom, and then another volunteer next to her, and on and on down the line.

"No! We're not done," I said. "We're not done!" I looked at Dad on one side of me and then at Mom on the other side. I was cold now, and tired. My shoes were wet, and bits of grass and seeds and prickly shrubbery had worked their way into my socks and through my jeans, scratching me. There was this ache in my chest that made it difficult to breathe. "We aren't done yet!" My voice cracked. I hadn't tried hard enough. This was all my fault, and I still hadn't fixed it. "We can't give up!"

"It's dark, sweetheart. We can't see anymore." Mom wrapped her arms around me.

I let go of my whistle. I hadn't even realized I'd been holding on to it—clenching my fist around it until it left an imprint in my palm. I wrapped my arms around Mom and rested my cheek against her shoulder. I blinked back tears. None of this would be happening right now if it hadn't been for me—for those words that had made my brother leave. What if we couldn't find him?

I took a shuddering breath. I'd listened and gathered clues and examined the evidence, but there was only silence.

"I'm sorry," I cried. "I'm so, so sorry."

Mom squeezed me tighter and tighter until I could feel her heart pounding against my chest.

"Shhh. This is no one's fault, Olivia." But she was crying, too. A second later, Dad wrapped his arms around us. The three of us cried together.

Officer Holtz came up behind us in the darkness. "We'll try again tomorrow, at first light." And the way she said it made me take a deep breath. She was firm. Reassuring. "If we try to search in the dark, we are guaranteed to miss something. We can't afford to miss a single thing."

Mom and Dad nodded. I wiped my eyes. She was right.

Officer Holtz radioed in and a few volunteers showed up with pickup trucks and four-wheelers to help give people rides back into town. Everyone piled in and shadows swam everywhere as we moved toward town.

Even though we were done for the night, I kept listening. I

listened so hard the inside of my head felt drawn tight, like a string on a guitar. Like it could snap any second if I wasn't careful. But I listened anyway. I listened and searched with every bit of myself, and still there was nothing. Not a sound. Not a whisper. Not even a breath.

I pictured Jacob's face in my mind. Narrow and freckled. Heavy dark eyebrows and a straight nose. I pictured the way he shifted his weight back and forth from one foot to the other when he was upset. And how he twisted his shirtsleeves. I pictured him staring just over my shoulder instead of meeting my eyes when he talked to me.

"It's okay," I whispered. "We're coming, Jacob. I'm coming. I won't stop looking."

Eventually, everyone gathered back together, the whole group of us, in the middle of our driveway. By this time all of our neighbors had heard about what was going on, and several of them walked over and stood in the yard with us, offering support and sympathy and help with whatever we could think to ask for.

Officer Blakeman stood up and whistled loudly with his fingers, calling for attention.

"We'll meet again in the morning, first light—six a.m. You're welcome to come back and help us pick up the search," he said to our neighbors. "But until then, there is little more you can do. Thank you all for your help this afternoon." He nodded to his officers and volunteers. And to Mom and Dad and me. "Every set of eyes matters. Thank you. Get some rest."

I watched as people left, our neighbors walking back across the street and through yards. So many people wanted to help. What would they say if they knew this was my fault?

I needed to hold it together. I needed to find Jacob.

I was the only one who could fix this. It couldn't wait till morning.

32

....

The Love Anyway

A COUPLE OF the officers stayed late to talk to Mom and Dad in the kitchen. They sat at the table and spread out maps. They pointed and said words like "topography" and "landscape," "direction" and "strategy." They circled places on the map and called them "zones," making plans for the morning. There were night officers out there in the dark now, searching with dogs, trying to pick up Jacob's scent. But so far none of the messages that came rattling and crackling through their radios had anything to do with finding my brother, and everything to do with still searching for him.

After they left, Mom and Dad sat next to each other on the couch in the living room, holding hands. They didn't say anything. They were just quiet. Staring at nothing. Staring at the empty place my brother had left behind.

"Mom? Dad?"

I stood in the middle of the living room, trying to decide what to say. How to say it.

"I have to tell you something," I said quietly. But the words were lodged in the back of my throat, stuck on the sob that forced its way out instead.

"Oh, sweetheart . . ." Mom stood up and held out her arms. I wanted nothing in the whole world as much as I wanted to just go and let her hug me and tell me it was all going to be okay. But I didn't. I shook my head and wrapped my arms around myself.

"This is all my fault," I choked.

"Honey, no." Dad shook his head and stood up beside Mom, but I interrupted him because he didn't really know. He didn't understand. Neither of them did. They were going to be mad. And disappointed. And I deserved that.

"When I told Jacob I *hated* him, and that he ruined everything, he believed me. He repeated it. And he slapped himself. Like this!" And I slapped myself, the way Jacob had in the middle of my room.

Mom wrapped her arms around me before I could do it again and kissed the slapped spot on my face.

"Shhh. I know, I know . . ." She held me there and rocked me until my breathing slowed down. Dad wrapped his arms around both of us. But they still didn't understand. They didn't know. They didn't know about my map, and searching for Jacob's ostrich, and my list of neverdos. They didn't know I knew about "Recurrence of Autism Spectrum Disorders in Siblings," and that I was like him.

"No. You don't."

They looked at me with questions.

"I know Jacob is getting worse. I've been looking for his missing ostrich—because that's when things started changing for him. When he lost it. He was different before it went missing. He was *better*!" I took a deep breath and kept going before they could stop me. "I even made a map so I could keep track of where I was searching. Then I found the article on Mom's desk," I said, my voice shaking. "I didn't mean to, but it was right there and I saw it. 'Recurrence of Autism Spectrum Disorders in Siblings.' And I know you think I have it. Just like Jacob. I'm trying really hard to keep from doing all the things Jacob does, but I end up doing them anyway. So, I've been looking and looking," I said, but I was crying now, too. "Because if I can just find Jacob's ostrich and give it back to him, I know it will help. I know it will make things better, like they were before. And if I can help Jacob, then maybe there's a way I can keep myself from getting worse, and then neither of us will need a change in environment or anything else."

I knew there was nothing that would make us normal, because "normal" wasn't even a thing. It was just the color green covering up the real colors underneath. I was crying so hard now I couldn't speak. But Mom and Dad squeezed me so tight and for so long that it didn't even matter.

The thing about telling the truth to the people who love the *you* underneath your skin, to the people who see your real deep-down colors, is that it doesn't change the love. That's what really matters. The love anyway. And I knew that more than anything—

more than missing ostriches and more than being "normal" and more than latent autism in siblings—we were a family.

And we weren't the same without Jacob.

I don't know how long we sat there in the living room before finally Mom kissed the top of my head and pulled away. She wiped tears off her cheeks and then mine, too.

"Sweetheart," she said, "I wish you'd told us about all of this sooner. Don't worry—we'll talk about the article. As for Jacob's ostrich—honey, that toy isn't lost. It never went missing. Your brother threw it away."

"What—?" I felt like I'd tripped and all the wind had been knocked out of me.

"He played with it so much that one day, it broke. One of the legs just snapped off. I tried to find one to replace it, but Jacob didn't want a new one. He wanted the old one. I superglued the leg back on, but it wouldn't stay, and it just kept making him more upset. So, when he said he didn't want it anymore, I let him get rid of it. I probably should have kept it, because later he missed it very much."

"But Jacob loved that ostrich. He should have kept it. Even if it was broken. It helped."

"What do you mean?" Dad asked. "Helped with what?"

"I . . . He was just . . . so much better before . . ." I thought I'd already cried all my tears, but suddenly there were more.

"Honey," Dad said, "Jacob was younger. And so were you! You both saw the world and understood things differently. The older Jacob gets, and the more complex life gets, the harder it is for him to process everything. And autism looks different on everyone. It can affect some people more complexly the older they get. It's not that he's worse, necessarily, or that he was better before, or that his toy has anything to do with it. It's just that you are both growing up. And when someone is autistic, growing up can be even harder."

I couldn't believe it. Everything was falling to pieces. If this wasn't something I could fix, if his toy ostrich had never really been missing, then Jacob had never needed me—never *wanted* me—to find it. No wonder I couldn't collect enough clues.

Then a much-worse thought struck me: What if Jacob himself didn't want to be found, either?

33

....

Tattoos

THE NIGHT SEARCH team didn't find any leads, so the next morning, a public service announcement was sent out about my brother. His description was on the radio, and both that and his picture were shown on TV.

Meanwhile, we continued to search the whole next day—Mom, Dad, and I, plus more volunteers, search dogs, neighbors, and other people we knew in Prue.

We walked and walked for miles, calling Jacob's name. I used every ounce of finding-lost-things talent I had. I took Jacob's picture from one of the frames in the living room and slipped it into my pocket. I wore his grey hoodie. I'd even slept on the floor in his room last night after Mom and Dad had gone to bed, trying to get as close to my brother as possible. But I knew it wouldn't help if Jacob didn't want to be found.

I'd never seen Mom and Dad like this. One minute they were calm, discussing plans and what to do next, and the next minute Mom was sitting down in the grass, her head in her hands, and Dad was on his knees beside her, rubbing her back and trying not to cry, too. I was trying to be brave for their sakes. But I was exhausted and sad and scared. My head ached and I felt sick to my stomach.

After a few hours, Mom and Dad sent me home to take a break. One of the officers took me back while they stayed out looking, and Charlie came over so I wouldn't be alone.

We sat together on the couch. He was quieter than usual.

"You warned me," I said. "I got too mad at him."

"I know," Charlie said.

"How did you know I might get upset and say something . . . terrible?" I asked.

There was a washcloth covering my forehead and eyes because I had a terrible headache. Charlie and I couldn't see each other. It was just our voices, real and truthy.

"I just know what it's like to say stuff you regret."

I had a hard time imagining Charlie saying anything hurtful to anyone. He was so good at making people feel better.

"I never really told you how I went blind," he said.

"You told me you were in an accident."

"I was. My mom was driving. We were coming back from a birthday party. It was raining and the car skidded out of control and hit a guardrail."

I took off the cloth so I could look at Charlie while he talked.

"The doctors said I hit my head—I honestly don't remember much about it—and it made my brain swell. A lot of pressure built up inside my head. I was in a coma for three days, and the swelling around my optic nerve permanently damaged my vision."

"Oh my goodness."

"I know. Pretty crazy, right? There was this one time about three years ago," Charlie continued, "when I was super mad about not being able to see and not being like a normal kid, and I said some things." Charlie cleared his throat. "To my mom."

"What kind of things?"

"I told her it was her fault," Charlie said. "That I was blind because of her." He paused. "It was the meanest thing I could think of to say. And it really hurt my mom to hear. I mean, yeah, it was a car accident and she was driving, but it's not like she made the road wet. Still, she felt like it was her fault somehow. And I knew that." He shrugged and his voice had gone very small.

I let out a breath.

"She said she felt like she had failed at being a mom because she didn't protect me."

"Wow," I said. "I—I'm so sorry."

"Things were hard for a while after that."

I nodded. I could imagine.

"Look, people who are hurting say and do hurtful things," he went on. "It was awful. But that whole thing taught me that when you hurt someone you love, either by accident or on purpose, you can always go back and work on the broken places. They might not look exactly like they did before, but they can be even better in the end. Stronger. That's why my mom has all those tattoos."

"What do you mean?" I asked.

"To remind us both that the things we do and say matter, and that it's important not to forget what we learn."

I tried to remember her tattoos, to picture them exactly. I remembered a birdcage with an open door. A lighthouse standing on a rock with waves rolling in around it. A pine tree tipped over on its side, roots pulling out of the ground. They were stories, I guess. Freedom and responsibility and a reminder that even strong trees fall. It was all written on her arms, where she could always see and remember.

Sometime during his talk, my tears had started up again. I sniffled and Charlie squeezed my hand.

"It's okay, Olivia," he said. "They'll find Jacob."

I squeezed his hand back. If only I could be so sure.

34

Through the Window

AFTER CHARLIE LEFT, I lay on the couch for the rest of the afternoon. I forced myself to imagine what life would be like if Jacob never returned. I didn't like what I saw.

Mom and Dad came back from searching around dinnertime with nothing new to report. They were quiet. The silence in the house that night was so heavy it felt like it was alive, pushing against the three of us like an invisible hand. I felt too sad and sick to eat, so I went to bed early.

Hours later, I sat up in bed, the slightest breath of a breeze pulling and pushing my curtains through my open window.

I could feel Ethel out in the yard even before I looked.

But this time there was no ostrich.

Instead, my brother was standing on the ground outside my window. I held my breath until I could hear my heart beating in my eardrums.

Jacob looked like a wild creature. He was covered in dirt, and there were twigs stuck to his clothes and bits of branches in his hair. In the moonlight, I could see scratches on his face and arms. His shirt was torn, and the wind pulled at the frayed edge. He was just standing there, perfectly still. Not looking in, exactly, but not looking anywhere else, either. He was waiting. Waiting to be let inside. Waiting for someone to tell him it was okay.

I crept out of bed very slowly. Carefully. My whole body was shaking. I wanted to call for Mom and Dad, but I was worried he would run away if I yelled.

"Jacob," I whispered. His name got lodged in my chest. "Jacob." I tried again, and this time his name came out, and I could tell he heard me.

He turned toward the window and met my eyes, just for a moment. And then he looked over my shoulder—the way he always did.

"Jacob, it's okay. You can come in." I whispered the words. I was so afraid of startling him. It was like he was a bird or wild creature, and I didn't want him to fly away. "Come in," I said again. "You can come in." I knelt by my open window.

Jacob just stood there. My lost and found brother. Wherever he'd been, he'd been hiding so well I bet no one ever would have found him. My stomach lurched and I reached out my window to him with both arms.

He shook his head. "I ruin everything," he said.

And a sob I didn't know I was holding fell out of me. My words. My horrible words sounded so much worse when Jacob said them back to me.

"I ruin everything. You hate me." He looked at me. "I hate me, too. Sometimes."

My heart felt like it was breaking apart. Tears made my vision swim.

"I'm sorry," I choked. "I'm so sorry, Jacob. It's not true. You don't ruin everything. I was upset and mean and wrong, and I'm sorry. But I'm not upset anymore and I'm not angry. Please come inside."

I was terrified he was going to run away and we'd never see him again. So, I stood up carefully and crawled over the windowsill, down into the grass. Jacob was even dirtier up close. And he was crying now, tears making tracks through the grime on his face.

Before I could stop myself, I hugged him. Gently at first, because Jacob didn't like to be touched. His body got tight and uncomfortable in my arms. But he didn't move, so I hugged him a little harder.

He didn't pull away.

I let my tears fall.

I cried because Jacob had come back all on his own, because he hadn't needed me to find him. I cried because suddenly, I felt like the lost one. I cried because I was sorry and because things were still broken and lost. I cried because of latent autism and neverdos and missing ostriches that had been broken and thrown away. I cried because Peter Pan had never known how much he was loved, and I'd almost missed the chance to tell my brother the same thing. I cried because Charlie would never see again, because I couldn't keep everything or everyone together no matter how hard I tried.

"Come on, Olivia," Jacob said finally. He pulled away from me, but he took my hand. And this time, I was the little sister for real. "I will take you home now," he said. And we both crawled back through my bedroom window.

After we went inside, and after I woke Mom and Dad, there was a lot more crying and hugging. Dad was crying and I was crying and Jacob was crying and moaning and starting to flail around because he didn't know what to do, and because everyone around him was upset. Mom was shaking and trying to hold on to my brother, who didn't want to be touched anymore that night.

Finally, we all took some deep breaths and tried to be calm for Jacob's sake.

Mom ran Jacob a bath, and Dad made hot chocolate and sandwiches (without the tops on them so that Jacob could put his sandwich together on his own), and my brother ate three of them after he got out of the tub.

Dad called the police who'd been working on Jacob's missing-persons case to let them know he had come home. It was very early in the morning, but they came anyway and tried to talk to my brother. They didn't get very far, of course. So, then they talked to me, and I just told them about waking up and finding Jacob standing there in the backyard, like a Lost Boy flown home from Neverland. It sounded silly, but I didn't care, because that's exactly how it felt.

The police talked to Mom and Dad about having the paramedics come to check out Jacob and make sure he was okay. Even though no one really wanted to make Jacob any more upset than he already was, it seemed like a good idea. So, the ambulance came, and the paramedics came, and there were more police cars in front of our house.

Slowly, lights starting coming on in our neighbors' windows, and a few people came over in their pajamas and slippers. Mrs. Mackenelli came with her hair in rollers, and when everyone found out what was going on—that Jacob had come home—there was more celebrating and crying.

It was the perfect picture of what being found looks like. Of celebrating what was lost, and wasn't lost anymore. And I realized something: Being loved is bigger, stronger, and more important than being lost. Being loved is what makes you valuable. It makes you worth searching for—no matter what. It's what makes it possible to be found. And Jacob, just like me, was worth finding.

35

·············

Changes

AFTER JACOB CAME home, Mom and Dad came up with a new plan. Ryan, Jacob's aide, would come to help with Jacob every weekday. He would arrive first thing in the morning and leave just before dinner.

He helped Jacob with a lot of things, and that helped Mom and Dad. It helped me, too. We all liked Ryan. He was funny, and he knew how to make Jacob relax. When Jacob couldn't be calmed down and started flailing and hitting and throwing things, Ryan was strong and calm, and he could help hold Jacob until he could be calm on his own. Ryan was like Jacob's bodyguard and teacher and mentor and big brother all rolled into one person. It was weird having him there so often at first, but it got less weird over time, and it was much better than giving Jacob a change in environment.

Dr. Kathy Martin came to evaluate Jacob more frequently, too. And she worked with the whole family to help us understand one another a little better—through games, questions, and even puzzles that were more about finding the picture than putting pieces together. Mom was super smart and had done lots of research on her own, but no one can do everything alone, and Dr. Kathy helped. She helped us talk about things in ways that Jacob could understand. And she gave us exercises to try so that when our family went places together, if Jacob started melting down over things like the color of the carpet or the number of chairs at a table, we didn't have to just leave. We could play a game about the things that made him uncomfortable, or distract him with something else, or take a walk.

Dr. Kathy also talked about us getting a dog for Jacob—and for us. A dog that would help him process his emotions in a way that he otherwise couldn't. A kind of special helper and friend—not just a pet. So, Mom and Dad were thinking about that.

Things were different between me and Mom and Dad, too. In some ways it seemed like they were just waking up. They were paying attention to me more and listening better. They understood it was important to me that I do my own things, too, so they were going to let me audition for another play. Plus, Mom was more open about her own stuff, too. She'd talk to me about things she'd just kept to herself before. About things that scared her, or things that made her excited. Sometimes they were things that scared or made me excited, too. And we started doing things together—shopping, going to the library or the zoo, or sometimes seeing a play in the city—just the two of us. Like she finally saw me.

I had finished my Responsibility Hours a few weeks earlier. I was glad to be finished, but sad, too, so I went back to the zoo one afternoon to see the animals and to visit Charlie. Just as I was getting ready to leave, I saw Mom standing at the entrance, waving at me.

"I thought it might be nice if we walked home together," Mom said. "And I got you a treat!" She handed me a package of Starburst. But I knew she was there for more than that, because her face was thoughtful and she was quieter than usual.

We weren't too far down the road when she stopped and pulled something out of her pocket.

"I wanted you to see this," she said. "*From me.*"

She handed me a piece of paper, and I felt my stomach sink as I unfolded it. It was that article I'd found on her desk: "Recurrence of Autism Spectrum Disorders in Siblings."

"I've already seen it," I said. I held it out for her to take back. I didn't want to read it. I never wanted to see it again. It was like a secret truth.

"I know," she said. "And I wish I could take that back, because I know it's caused you pain." Mom's voice was tight. "I wanted to make sure I had more information before I talked to you about it. And then things got a little crazy."

I couldn't look at her.

"Olivia, I don't think you're autistic. I never did."

The ground under my feet began to sway.

"But . . . then why did you have this article on your desk?"

Mom just shook her head. "I wasn't reading it because of you and Jacob, specifically. There are new findings and there's new research being done about autism all the time. It's my job as your mom to read as much as I can, and to try to learn as much as possible so I can help your brother, and you, and me . . ." She paused. "Olivia, did you know Uncle Dan is autistic, too?"

I frowned. My uncle Dan was always a little different, but he was super nice. He played the guitar better than anyone else I knew, and whenever he came to visit, he brought it along and played for us. But I never thought . . .

"So—so you weren't worried about me?"

"Yes and no. I wasn't worried about you because I thought you were autistic, but because I was interested in how autism affects genetics. And I wanted to know how latent autism could possibly affect *me*." Her face flushed, like she'd told me a secret. Her secret fear—the same as mine. I'd just never known. My heart was racing.

"But why would you be worried about *yourself*? You're not autistic!"

Mom smiled. "Well, why would you be worried about *your*self, Olivia? You're not autistic, either."

"But—" I paused and stared at her for a minute.

"And Olivia," she continued, "even if you were autistic, even if you *are*, it doesn't matter. It doesn't change the way I feel about you, or the way Dad feels about you, or the way Jacob feels about you. You will always be who you are, no matter what. The world is full of many different kinds of people. That's what makes life beautiful and interesting."

A lump was forming in my throat again. I didn't know what to say. Before I could even try, Mom took the article from my hands and held it up. And then, right there on the minimal maintenance road, she ripped it down the middle. She handed me half, and together we each ripped up our piece into smaller pieces, over and over until the wind took them away.

Big things made smaller.

For all of us.

36

....

A Plan

DESPITE EVERYTHING, ONE thing didn't change, and that was Ethel. She found her way to my backyard a few days after Jacob came back home, and then again the week after, until finally I had to do something.

Charlie and I still hadn't told anyone else about Ethel escaping to my backyard, and now that my Responsibility Hours were over, and the renovations at the zoo in Tulsa were almost finished, and our little portion of the zoo would be leaving in a week, it seemed a little late to do so. Especially because nothing ever happened once she got out. But I wanted to solve the mystery. Charlie did, too.

"So, I think I have a plan," he said. We were standing in front of Ethel's enclosure. Even though I didn't have to be at the zoo, I wanted to be.

"You do?" I handed Charlie a Starburst, and he unwrapped it and popped it into his mouth.

"Yep. But I'm going to need your help."

"Well, I figured that much."

He laughed.

"So . . . what is it?" I asked.

"It involves sneaking into the zoo." He paused. "In the middle of the night."

I stared at him. It was risky enough to return Ethel to the zoo after hours. But sneaking in without her?

"You *do* know that's what got me into trouble in the first place, right?"

Charlie nodded and grinned. "But it's kind of fitting, right? Like, full circle."

"Full circle?"

"Yeah. You started this summer by trespassing on zoo property. It only seems right that you should finish the summer the same way."

"Are you joking?"

"No! I swear. And it will be different this time because I'll be there, too, and I'm the zookeeper's son. I *can't* get in trouble. Plus, it's not technically trespassing if I let you in."

I thought about that for a second. "What's the actual plan, though?" I unwrapped another Starburst. A yellow one.

"You've got to get here before Ethel ends up in your back-yard," Charlie said.

"You mean, so we can see who's letting her out?"

"Exactly."

Goose bumps ran up and down my arms.

"But what if we get caught?"

"By who? My mom?"

"I don't know. By whoever's letting Ethel out of her cage. What if that person is, like, a criminal or dangerous or something?"

"We won't get caught. And we won't actually do anything. We're just going to hide and wait. And once we know who's been letting Ethel out of her cage, we can report them."

It seemed like a great idea, except that there was no pattern to Ethel's trips to my backyard. Sometimes it was once a week, sometimes more often. The only thing that never seemed to change was the time. Aside from that first night, I always woke up a few minutes after midnight and there she was. So, Charlie and I had to be at the zoo, hidden somewhere near Ethel's enclosure before midnight, every night, until we caught whoever was letting her out.

I just hoped we could figure it out before the zoo left town.

37

The Ostrich Bandit

THAT NIGHT, I set my alarm clock for 11:30 p.m.

My backpack was under my bed, packed full of snacks, my black hoodie, a flashlight, ostrich food from the zoo—just in case I needed to lure Ethel back into her cage or something—and a package of Starburst. For luck.

When my alarm went off, I crept out of bed, pulled on a pair of dark jeans and a black T-shirt, and grabbed my backpack. Then I whispered to Mom and Dad to tell them where I was going, and slipped out my open window.

It was one thing to walk down the minimal maintenance road with an ostrich in the middle of the night. I didn't have the time to be nervous or afraid of little night critters in the grass or owls flying above me. But now, alone, I was freaked out by any rustling in the grass or whisper of wings overhead. I hurried as fast as I could.

By the time I got to the gate, I was out of breath. The plan was for Charlie to let me in, so I was super relieved to see him slip out of the shadows when I got there.

"Welcome to the Prue Zoo," Charlie whispered. He unlocked the gate and let me inside. "Please don't feed the animals while you're here."

I laughed nervously. We walked quietly to where Ethel waited in her enclosure. Closer and closer, with careful steps. As we settled down behind some hay bales, ready to wait, she ruffled her feathers and opened her eyes. Now she was staring at us like we were crazy. Maybe we were. But it was exciting and scary and adventurous.

I was glad Charlie was there with me. We had no guarantee that tonight would be the night the Ostrich Bandit would show up, but we had to start somewhere. So, with the rasping chirp of crickets in the warm darkness all around us, the muffled noises of a giant bird reminding us of our mission, and Starburst to keep us awake, Charlie and I sat in the dark behind a couple bales of hay next to Ethel's enclosure. And we waited.

Every huff and ruffle of feathers made us freeze. The occasional screech of a monkey or the stomping hoof of a donkey made a cold sweat break out on the back of my neck. But soon those noises became familiar, and Charlie and I talked in almost silent whispers. He told me about his school, about classes and teachers and about reading in braille. I told him about school in Prue and how I was a little nervous about going into seventh grade and making friends. And about Jacob—whether he'd be able to make friends and do okay in class, even with Ryan's help.

"Charlie?" I whispered.

"Yeah?"

"Thanks for helping me. And for being my friend and stuff."

He laughed and squeezed my hand. And everything smelled like pink Starburst.

The Ostrich Bandit didn't come that night. We only had six days left to figure out who was letting Ethel out. So, Charlie and I kept watch over her enclosure, night after night, waiting for a sign, whispering as quietly as possible, jumping at unfamiliar sounds, and sometimes holding hands. When the sky started turning grey with the approaching sunrise, we would get up and tiptoe through the crunchy gravel. Charlie would let me back through the gate before locking it behind me. And then we would both sneak back to our own houses in time to change clothes and rub our eyes before any of the grown-ups were awake. It was tiring, and after the third night, I was ready to give up. I could barely stay awake through breakfast, and my parents noticed.

But on the fourth night, everything changed. Charlie nudged me awake in the darkness outside Ethel's enclosure.

"Someone's coming!" His voice was urgent.

I froze in the darkness. My heart leapt into my throat.

This was it.

Charlie and I both rolled over onto our stomachs, and I peered into the darkness. This part was my job. I was the only one who'd be able to identify the Ostrich Bandit, and I needed a good look.

Crunch, crunch, crunch, crunch.

Someone was walking toward Ethel's cage. My breath came faster and faster. My heart was pounding so hard in my chest that Charlie could probably hear it.

"Can you see anything?" he whispered.

"Not yet."

The footsteps came closer and closer, and Ethel perked up in her cage, ruffled her feathers, and bobbed her head. She knew what happened next. And so did I. Someone was about to let her out.

A dark figure rounded the corner and walked only a couple feet in front of where Charlie and I were hidden behind some hay bales.

I couldn't see who it was at first. And then, little pieces of things I'd wondered about over the past couple weeks—things that had been waiting at the corners of my mind—began to make sense.

Him standing in the living room in the middle of the night when I found the latent autism article.

The Cap'n Crunch in the pocket of his hoodie.

As I stayed there with Charlie, I watched as my brother—*my brother, Jacob*—pulled something from his pocket.

Keys.

The ones Phil had lost weeks ago. Somehow, my brother had them. And I continued to watch as he unlocked Ethel's enclosure, swung the door open, and ushered her out into the courtyard.

38

All Along

"JACOB!" I SAID his name louder than I meant to. But I was tired and upset and couldn't believe what I was seeing.

Jacob yelped and spun around, and Ethel did this funny little hop straight into the air, then bolted to the other side of the courtyard. Thank heavens the main gate was closed, or she would have been halfway across Oklahoma.

If you've never seen an ostrich run, it's really the most astonishing thing. Their necks stay mostly upright—unlike a horse or another four-legged creature that stretches into their run. Ostriches are very dignified about it. They take giant fluid stretches that eat up great swaths of space beneath them. Their wings arch out from their bodies a little bit, and they flutter them at their sides. Not like they're flapping or trying to fly, more like testing the air—testing the space around their bodies—so they can run more freely.

Ethel ran, testing the air with her wings, all around the courtyard. My brother started wailing. Charlie stood pressed against the wall of the building beside Ethel's enclosure, trying to stay clear of a bolting ostrich he couldn't see. I called and called for Jacob to get out of the way. And then Vera was there in her pajamas, with a flashlight that was truly blinding when it hit your eyes.

It wasn't exactly how I had pictured solving the mystery of the escaping ostrich. Especially when dust started flying everywhere and gravel sprayed up from under Ethel's feet. The chaos of it all frightened more than just Jacob, and Charlie, and me—the other animals went nuts, too.

The monkeys started screeching and the donkeys started braying. I couldn't do anything except stand there helplessly while Vera took charge.

"Olivia, grab your brother and head to our trailer!"

Then she took Charlie by the arm, and I ran toward Jacob. We made our way across the parking lot, up the stairs, and into the trailer where Vera and Charlie lived. And then we all sat, breathless, while the sun came up and Ethel ran back and forth from one end of the courtyard to the other.

"*What. On earth. Were you doing?!*" Vera wasn't quite speechless, but almost. And mad. I bet she'd never imagined this small portion of the Tulsa Zoo in the tiny town of Prue, Oklahoma, was going to be so much work.

"I can explain—" Charlie began.

"It's my fault—" I interrupted.

Jacob just wailed.

Vera held up her hands for silence, and even Jacob listened.

The tattoos on her arms caught his attention, and he actually stopped crying.

"Why is the ostrich out of her cage?" Vera was trying very hard to be calm. It was kind of impressive. "Olivia, have you been letting her out this entire time?" She looked straight at me, and I felt my mouth drop open.

"Of course not!" Charlie answered for me. "She's been the one bringing Ethel back home!"

"What do you mean, bringing her home?" Vera turned on Charlie, who suddenly clapped his hands over his mouth. No one had said anything about Ethel getting past the main gate. Vera didn't know that part. "What does he mean, *bringing her home*, Olivia?" Vera repeated.

"Um . . . Jacob has been letting her out. And . . ." I cleared my throat, trying to explain this in a way that wouldn't require me to give away all the details. But there was really no way to tell a zoo-keeper that her ostrich had been escaping all summer without just saying her ostrich had been escaping all summer. So, Charlie and I told her everything.

"But we didn't know Jacob was the one letting her out until tonight!"

Vera's face was very white and her eyes were wide. Even Charlie looked scared of her.

"This has been going on *all summer*?!" Her voice sounded tight and even deeper than usual.

I nodded. A very tiny nod.

"Why didn't you ever say anything? Phil and I have been trying to figure out how Ethel was getting out of her cage for the past several weeks! He told me he'd lost a set of keys, but we never made the connection. Did Jacob have them this whole time?"

I shrugged.

"Olivia, why wouldn't you tell me?!"

Her voice wasn't small anymore, and I sank into the couch cushions, wishing I could disappear.

"At first I was afraid you wouldn't believe me if I told you it wasn't me who'd let her out. And then when it kept happening, I was afraid you'd be mad at me for not saying anything sooner."

"Yes. Well, you were correct." Vera covered her face with her hands and scrubbed them back through her hair. "You should have told me the moment you discovered an ostrich in your backyard! And Charlie! You knew and you never said anything, either?"

She looked from me to Charlie and back again.

"Do you both realize I could lose my job over this?"

I didn't know what to say. Charlie and I were both quiet, and there were tears rising behind my eyes. I blinked multiple times and clamped my lips together to keep from crying.

"And you!" Vera turned to Jacob, who refused to look at her and instead stared off toward the wall over her shoulder. He was rocking and twisting the sleeves on his hoodie.

Vera knelt down in front of him. "What were you thinking,

Jacob?" Her voice was softer because she knew about my brother, but I don't think she fully understood until that moment. "Why did you let Ethel out of her cage? Why would you do that? Do you know how dangerous that was? Ethel is pretty tame, but even tame animals can hurt you!"

She pleaded with him for an explanation. Wanting to know what we all were desperate to understand.

My brother stayed silent, rocking and twisting his sleeves, his face shifting between frustration and confusion and pleading, and I really didn't think he was going to say anything. But then he did.

"I did it for Olivia," he said. But he didn't look at me. He just rocked. "She is Olivia's ostrich. And mine."

"Jacob . . . Ethel isn't my ostrich . . . *or* yours." I didn't understand. But I wanted to. I really did. So, I took a deep breath. "Can you say it a different way?" My voice caught in my throat. That was one of the phrases Dr. Kathy had told us to try when we didn't understand what Jacob was trying to explain.

Jacob rocked and rocked.

"You—you were looking for my ostrich," he said. He shook his head and pressed his fists into his hair, frustrated with himself, and then he started again. His words were halted and he frowned a lot, trying to make them come out right. "You find lost things. You were looking and looking, but my ostrich was not lost." He looked at me and then looked away again. "I am not lost, either . . ." He thumped his chest with the palm of his hand. Three times.

My eyes started to water.

"It's okay, Olivia," my brother said. And he reached out and patted my shoulder. "Don't be sad, Olivia. I am okay."

I covered my face with my hands and cried because I knew he was right.

I finally understood.

All this time, Jacob knew I was looking for his ostrich—that toy he threw away—because I thought it would fix something that wasn't actually broken, find something that wasn't ever lost. All summer he had brought Ethel home for me. He'd been trying to tell me that everything was okay all along. *I* was the one who hadn't understood what he was saying. I thought I had been the one helping Jacob when really, my brother had been the one helping me.

39

··············

Found

THAT SUMMER IT took my brother, a temporary zoo, Peter Pan, an ostrich, all the colors—visible and invisible—my friend Charlie, a bit of mapmaking, autism, and a whole lot of searching before I finally came to understand that there really is no such thing as normal. That we are all a little bit lost and a little bit found, and that both of those things are beautiful.

Jacob didn't magically get better as summer drew to a close and school started again. If anything, he kept growing up and getting more complicated. But Mom and Dad and I got better at being patient and asking questions in a different way, and loving him and each other.

Mom and Dad weren't too happy when they found out I'd been sneaking out of the house all summer long to bring Ethel back to the zoo. Discovering there'd been an ostrich in the backyard throughout the summer was bad enough. And they were pretty freaked out when they found out Jacob had been leaving the house, too. They made me promise not to leave the house, by means of the window or the chimney or any other way, without telling them first—and *not* in quiet whispers outside their bedroom door while they were sleeping. To their faces when they were awake. So, I wouldn't. But I still kept my window open at night.

As for Jacob, Mom and Dad made him start wearing a special bracelet that's a kind of tracking device, just in case he ever ran away again or got lost. It was a safety precaution. He actually thought it was pretty cool and showed it to people. "Did you know I have a superpower bracelet?" he'd say. "You can find me anywhere in the world."

Prue's portion of the zoo went back to Tulsa the last week in August, just before school started. Charlie and Vera went with it, along with Phil, Bridget, and Maggie.

It was hard to say goodbye to Charlie, but we promised to stay in touch. He hugged me for a long time, and I knew he was saying things about loving, and being real, and no such thing as normal, and being found.

I hugged him long and hard right back.

I gave Charlie a special goodbye present, too. I bought a bunch of packages of Starburst and took out all the pink ones before carefully wrapping only those back up and taping the package shut. I knew he would understand.

Charlie and my brother and an ostrich had shown me how to look inside people, where they were the most real, the most lost, and to love them anyway. They taught me that we're all *all the colors*, and that if you insist on pretending to be anything else, you'll never be found and loved all the way. Not really.

As for me, I was a finder of lost things and a lover of found things. I was learning to be brave, even when I was scared, and I was learning that I could be Jacob's sister and still be Olivia, too. That those things might be different at times, but that I was always still me, whether I was acting in a play, or hanging out with Jacob, or spending time with Charlie, or studying at school, or doing anything anywhere and everywhere else.

Most of all, I was learning to love, even when it was hard. Because, after all, there's nothing more important than that.

Author's Note

This book is not meant to be a commentary on autism or some kind of fictional discussion of the vast array of spectrum disorders. In fact, the field of study continues to expand in areas of autism, Asperger's, and spectrum disorders faster than I could ever hope to follow, much less write about.

If you have read this story, and you yourself are on the spectrum, or you love someone who is, please know there were times as I wrote this tale that I intentionally challenged Olivia's ability to show empathy. She had a lot of learning and growing to do.

Olivia's story is merely a glimpse through a keyhole into an imagined life. One tiny picture of what it might be like to learn how to love better. Both others and self. And this is a difficult thing for each one of us, no matter where we land on the spectrum.

As this story came to be, people I love dearly—those with intimate personal experience, and those with professional medical experience—came to my aid in its telling. They steadied me where my lack of experience and understanding failed. They corrected my errors with grace and kindness. They helped me shape the fictional characters in this book with greater depth. And in so doing, they let me into their own experiences. They shared their stories and their hearts. They opened their homes to me, and they took off their masks. And for that I am forever grateful. I know my telling of this tale isn't perfect. Perhaps you will find places where I got it wrong. Because I am still learning, too.

To those on the spectrum, to those with disabilities, to those misdiagnosed, to those on the edge of breakthrough, and to all those who hold their hearts and walk this difficult road with them: You are so brave.

Thank you for letting me tell a story that doesn't look away.

Acknowledgments

Writing a book (like directing a play, or running a zoo, or raising a child) is never a one-person job. It takes a team. And mine has been fantastic, offering cues from the wings, making sure all the animals are in their cages at night, and cutting off sandwich crusts (figuratively speaking) as this story came to life. I couldn't have done this without them.

Thank you to my family: my husband, Aaron, and our kids, Caleb, Ella, Lucy, and June. You all continue to give me perspective and lend texture to my writing endeavors. You also continually bring me back to what truly matters in life by teaching me how to love better and how to be brave, day in and day out.

Thank you to my parents, who read and applaud and believe no matter what. And thanks to my sisters, to whom this book is dedicated. We don't get to pick our family, but had I been given the option, I would have chosen all of you.

Thank you to Dr. Monica Goodwin, MD, and your family. And Dr. Stephanie Parrish, OD. You both offered medical expertise and knowledge, answered questions, and helped me sort out details that I couldn't have understood on my own. Thank you for helping to make both Jacob and Charlie come alive on the page.

Thanks to Jolene L., who read and offered so much encouragement; Jodi C., who read and prayed while she cut my hair; Katie, for reading and listening; Jodi S., for being my first set of editorial eyes (I'd never be where I am today without you); and Angela, who is always reading and cheering for me (page 3 belongs to you, girl!). Thanks to Kelley, Leah, Sarah, Liz, Tab, Kara, Jill, Megan, and all the women in our book club. Doing life with all of you saves me more often than you know! And to Caitlin, Grace, and Paige: You have been there so often to play with my children as I pounded words against the page. You are caretakers of my precious Littles, and "thank you" doesn't go far enough.

I am a better woman because I have you all in my life. Thank you for being my people.

And thanks to the rest—families who will go unnamed here for the sake of respecting your privacy. Your stories and your hard work, carried out with love and courage, will never be fully recognized for what it is. But you are changing the world, one kid at a time. I am honored to know you. Forgive the parts of this story that have oversimplified or glossed over the vast breadth of what it means to work and parent as you do, going about life through difficult challenges. I hope I have at least given the world a glimpse.

Thanks to the team of dream-makers at Philomel/Penguin Random House: Michael Green, Tony Sahara, David Briggs, Talia

Benamy, and especially Liza Kaplan. Thank you for editing, advising, and encouraging with sensitivity, kindness, and extraordinary skill. I couldn't have done this without you.

Thank you to my agent, Danielle, and the good people at Upstart Crow for believing that this was a story worth telling, and that I was the one to tell it. Your belief makes me able.

And finally, my lifelong gratitude to my Heavenly Father, who didn't leave me lost.